"I want to hate you, Cat."

Luke's words were angry. "But I can't, and I just don't understand it. I feel as if I were lost in a maze of mirrors—I can't seperate the false image from the true path out."

"I can tell you what's true," she said quickly. "I can explain...."

He swung around to face her with an expression that had hardened into bitterness.

"Explain what?" he asked curtly. "And whose truth will you tell me, Cat? What image will I get this time?"

"Stop it," she said sharply. Tears of anger and frustration slid down her cheeks. She inhaled deeply and tried to steady her voice. "Why do you... how can you assume the worst about me?"

"Why are you still wearing his wedding ring?" he countered.

SANDRA MARTON says she's always believed in romance. She wrote her first love story when she was nine and fell madly in love at sixteen with the man who is her husband. Today they live on Long Island, midway between the glitter of Manhattan and the quiet beaches of the Atlantic. Sandra is delighted to be writing the kinds of stories she loves and even happier to find that her readers enjoy them, too.

Books by Sandra Marton

HARLEQUIN PRESENTS

988—A GAME OF DECEIT
1027—OUT OF THE SHADOWS
1067—INTIMATE STRANGERS
1082—LOVESCENES
1121—HEART OF THE HAWK
1155—A FLOOD OF SWEET FIRE
1194—DEAL WITH THE DEVIL
1219—CHERISH THE FLAME
1244—EYE OF THE STORM
1277—FLY LIKE AN EAGLE

Don't miss any of our special offers. Write to us at the following address for information on our newest releases.

Harlequin Reader Service
901 Fuhrmann Blvd., P.O. Box 1397, Buffalo, NY 14240
Canadian address: P.O. Box 603,
Fort Erie, Ont. L2A 5X3

SANDRA MARTON

from this day forward

Harlequin Books

TORONTO • NEW YORK • LONDON
AMSTERDAM • PARIS • SYDNEY • HAMBURG
STOCKHOLM • ATHENS • TOKYO • MILAN

Harlequin Presents first edition October 1990
ISBN 0-373-11308-0

Original hardcover edition published in 1985
by Mills & Boon Limited

Copyright © 1985 by Sandra Marton. All rights reserved.
Except for use in any review, the reproduction or utilization
of this work in whole or in part in any form by any electronic,
mechanical or other means, now known or hereafter invented,
including xerography, photocopying and recording,
or in any information storage or retrieval system, is forbidden without
the permission of the publisher, Harlequin Enterprises Limited,
225 Duncan Mill Road, Don Mills, Ontario, Canada M3B 3K9.

All the characters in this book have no existence outside the
imagination of the author and have no relation whatsoever to
anyone bearing the same name or names. They are not even
distantly inspired by any individual known or unknown to the
author, and all incidents are pure invention.

® are Trademarks registered in the United States Patent and
Trademark Office and in other countries.

Printed in U.S.A.

CHAPTER ONE

IT was that most perfect time of day, the moment when twilight becomes night, and the sky over Paris was bathed in vivid streaks of sapphire against a pale wash of blue. Along the elegant Avenue George V, the streetlights winked on like fireflies, adding a glittering touch of brightness to the early spring evening. The broad avenue was filled with pedestrians and cars, all hurrying homeward while the city shed her daytime garb for the more tantalising cloak of evening. There was, as always, an air of excitement in the streets, a sense of romance and unexpected encounters, but the young woman bent over a stack of computer printouts in a small conference room inside the Hotel George V was unaware of it. In fact, it was only when her secretary sighed wearily, got up from her chair and switched on the lights that Caitlin Thomas noticed that the handsome room had begun to grow dark. She looked up, her face a pale oval against the rich chestnut of her hair, and smiled.

'Thank you, Jean,' she said, tiredly flexing her shoulders. 'These figures were getting hard to see. I'd begun to think I needed glasses.'

Jean Barrows clucked her tongue in amusement and grinned.

'What would you do without me, Caitlin? I take your dictation, organise your office, and now I even solve your medical problems. If I could only convince you not to work so hard, I'd be satisfied.'

Caitlin closed the folder and pushed it aside. 'I'm

sorry, Jean, the time kind of slipped away from me. You must be exhausted.'

'I'm all right, Caitlin. You're the one who should be in a state of collapse by now. You must have those figures memorised; we've been over them at least four times since we got here yesterday. Don't you think it's time you took a break?'

'I just want to check one last thing,' Caitlin said, reaching for her half-filled coffee cup. 'If those profit margins are as inflated as they appear to be ...' She paused and sipped at the murky liquid. 'Ugh, this is awful. It tastes like mud.'

'Coffee usually tastes like that when it's cold,' her secretary said pointedly. 'That stuff's been sitting there since lunch, for heaven's sake. I'll order a fresh pot.'

Caitlin shook her head and grimaced as she gulped down the remaining coffee. 'No, don't bother. I'll have some sent to my suite later when I order dinner.'

'Don't tell me you're going to eat in your room again tonight,' she said slowly. 'This is Paris, after all. You know, the city of light, the city for lovers. Didn't you read any of those travel brochures I kept piling on your desk before we left California? And what about that nice man, the Marquis of Whatsit, you know the one I mean, Caitlin, the guy who came to the office last winter. I gave you his messages, didn't I?' she asked worriedly. 'I'm sure I did. He phoned yesterday, and today, too, asking you to please call him. He said he wants to take you to dinner. I know I gave you those memos,' she added, rummaging through a stack of papers.

Caitlin's green eyes lit with amusement. 'Of course you did, Jean. I just don't have the time to see him. Don't make a face. I promise, I'll phone him next week, before we fly home, and make my apologies.' She smiled wryly. 'I know you won't let me forget.'

'Come on, Caitlin, why don't you break down and go out with the guy? I bet he'd take you on a tour of Paris you'd never forget.'

'You're probably right. But there simply isn't any time to spare. The stockholders' meeting is coming up in a few days, and I'm more and more convinced that this merger with Evian et Frères is a bad idea.' Caitlin sighed and tapped her fingers on the stacked computer printouts. 'Somewhere in here are the facts I need to convince the others. If we can just ferret them out . . .'

'No matter what you dredge up, you're never going to persuade your aunt Emily and her son to vote against the merger. Well, it's the truth,' Jean added defensively when her employer frowned. 'So why not sit back, relax, and just wait for your cousins' proxy votes to get here? Forget you're the head of Thomas Pharmaceuticals for a little while.' She walked to the window and pulled aside the heavy curtains. 'Just look at that city out there. Doesn't it make you want to pretend you're just a tourist, at least for a day or two?'

A dark shadow seemed to dull Caitlin's eyes and she smiled wistfully. 'It makes me want to pretend a lot of things,' she murmured. She stared out of the window for a moment and then shook her head and turned away. 'But I'm not here to play games,' she said briskly. 'And it certainly wasn't my idea to hold this meeting in Paris. Well,' she added in a lighter tone, 'that's the price you pay when a company is family owned. The others simply outvoted me, so here I am.'

'And what good is it doing you? When I think of what I would have given to have had an all-expenses-paid trip to Paris when I was your age . . . lunch at Maxim's, shopping at Le Printemps, dinner at La Tour d'Argent . . . aren't you just aching to do those things?'

Caitlin grinned and leaned back in her chair. 'Well,

at least one of us has been reading those brochures. Actually, my list is a little different. I'd love to see some of the museums—the Louvre, certainly—and then the Tuileries Gardens, and the Eiffel Tower, and ...' Her smile faded and she began leafing through the printouts. 'I'll see how much time I have left after I finish with this.'

'You'll make the time,' Jean said cheerfully. 'I'll see to that.'

There was a companionable silence in the room for several minutes, broken only by the rustle of paper and the scratch of Jean's pen. Then, she chuckled and smiled slyly at Caitlin.

'I guess you didn't completely ignore those travel brochures, did you?'

'Oh, I took a look at them. And even if I hadn't,' Caitlin added quietly, gazing out of the window, 'I'd know the names of those places. I used to dream about coming to Paris years ago. Sometimes, I felt as if I knew the city without ever having set foot in it. And this was the time of year I wanted to be in France,' she added, her eyes fixed unseeingly on the street outside. 'Warm days, cool nights—and there are poppy fields in bloom in the countryside right now. I saw a painting of them once ... row after row of bright crimson flowers. So beautiful ...' Caitlin's voice drifted off into silence and she smiled apologetically. 'You see?' she said briskly. 'Not even I can resist *La Belle France*. Here I am, starting to sound like an advertisement for the tourist office, and I've still got all this work to do.'

'Well, that's a surprise,' Jean said slowly, watching Caitlin's face with great care. 'Was that a trip you planned with your husband before he died? Nobody dreams about Paris alone.'

'With Justin?' Caitlin smiled and shook her head.

'No, it was long ago, before I married him, before . . .' Abruptly, she rose from her chair, strode briskly to the window, and drew the curtains. 'We'll never finish up at this rate,' she said, turning back to the desk and the papers strewn across it. She glanced at her watch and then picked up one of the computer printouts. 'I know it's late, but I'd like to go through these figures one last time so that you can make some notes for me. Then tonight, I'll be able to check the details myself. Can you stay for another half-hour or so, Jean? If you have other plans, I can always dictate what I need to the tape recorder.'

'I wish I did have other plans,' Jean said wistfully, a look of regret on her plain face. 'I can stay, of course. I'd planned on taking my trusty guidebook and going for a walk along the Champs Elysées—maybe stop for dinner at one of those cute little cafés. But it's still early. They say Paris doesn't really get going until late, although I haven't figured out what that means in my case.' Caitlin smiled and Jean grinned at her. 'Okay, which figures are we going over this time? The ones from last year?'

Caitlin nodded and began to make pencilled notations on the printout. 'Yes, those are the ones that seem most inflated. Just take down these numbers and some ideas that I have about them.'

The two women worked quietly for the next twenty minutes, oblivious to the noise of traffic drifting in from the street and the muffled sounds of other hotel guests in the corridor. Finally, Caitlin sighed and tossed aside her pencil.

'Well, that does it for tonight,' she said, closing the folder in front of her. 'Thanks for staying so late, Jean. I know you must be aching to get out of here and have dinner, but I need all the ammunition I can muster for that meeting.'

'My money's on you, Caitlin,' her secretary answered, gathering the papers together neatly and placing them in a leather case. 'I'm not very good at all this, but even I can see that something's wrong with these profit and loss statements.'

Caitlin got to her feet and took her grey wool suit jacket from the back of the chair. 'Yes, but you aren't Emily Thomas,' she said, smoothing down her raw silk blouse before slipping her arms into the jacket. 'All Aunt Emily can see is how much money she might make if this merger goes through. It won't really matter to her that Evian isn't all it claims. And I know better than to mention that they make some of their money by limiting the production of their newer drugs. The last time I said something like that,' she added, laughing at the memory, 'Emily all but accused me of being a bleeding-heart lunatic. All that counts is how much she gets in her dividend cheque.'

'She can't complain about that. You've got to admit the company's been turning a nice profit for the four years you've been running it. Besides, these people are family. They'll listen to you.'

Caitlin gathered some papers together and stuffed them into her briefcase. 'They're Justin's relatives, not mine. Even before I became director, or married Justin, Emily seemed uncomfortable having me present at meetings.'

'You owned—what was it—five percent of the stock then in your own right, didn't you?'

Caitlin smiled, nodding in agreement. 'Emily never said anything, but she resented that. Justin's father always felt that my dad gave Thomas Pharmaceuticals its first step up. If he hadn't discovered one of the first synthetic steroid compounds, the company wouldn't have survived its first couple of years. He left my father those shares in his will, and when my dad passed on, the stock became mine.'

'Then nobody, including Emily Thomas, had a right to object,' Jean said.

'I'm afraid she didn't see it quite that way. You see, my dad never voted his stock, or attended meetings. But when I inherited it, I was already working at Thomas, and I was really interested in the company. I wanted . . .' Caitlin's voice trailed off in mid-sentence and she seemed to gather herself together. 'Anyway, that's past history,' she said, almost brusquely. 'All that matters is getting through the meeting next week. And I don't want to make any mistakes, Jean. Sometimes, I think Emily and one or two of the others have been waiting for me to do just that.'

'You haven't yet,' Jean said with an impish grin.

'Yes, but this is different. This merger would be kind of glamorous, after all. International connections, French branch offices . . .' Caitlin looked up and smiled. 'All this talk of making a château outside Paris into a European headquarters is pretty high-powered stuff.'

'You know,' Jean said, choosing her words carefully, 'you could just let the merger go through and avoid the fight. Those people at Clarke Labs still want you as director. Big job, big company, more money, stock options . . .'

Caitlin shook her head and closed her briefcase. 'I gave them my answer last week,' she said firmly. 'I'm not the least bit interested in that position. I'd have to sell my shares in Thomas, and I'm not about to let Emily or anyone else ruin it.'

'But . . .'

'No "buts",' Caitlin said quickly. 'And no more talk about work. Just listen to me, prattling on about my problems, and here you are, starved, overworked, exhausted . . .'

Jean started to chuckle. 'How about underpaid? Well, I thought, as long as you were feeling guilty, I'd give it my best shot.' She walked to the door and then turned to face Caitlin. 'I know it's useless to ask you to call that Frenchman—after all, you hardly ever go out with anybody back home, so why should I expect miracles here—but, well, if you want company, you're more than welcome to tag along with me this evening. I know that Paris is made for lovers, not lady tourists, but you, me, and my Michelin guidebook have got to be better than another evening spent cuddled up with room service and yards of computer printouts.'

'I can't thank you enough for inviting me, but I really have work to do—you know that. You just go on and have a nice evening, and then tomorrow, you can tell me about everything I missed.'

'You're going to hate yourself for turning down a date with that Frenchman,' Jean grumbled good-naturedly as she opened the door. 'A marquis, for goodness sakes,' she added, making a face. 'How come these things never happen to me?'

Caitlin laughed at her secretary. 'See you in the morning,' she said cheerfully.

Once the door had closed, her smile faded and she slumped back wearily into the chair by the desk, sighed and closed her eyes. She was almost as much a puzzle to her secretary as she was to others, she thought. Jean had come to work at Thomas Pharmaceuticals shortly after Caitlin became its director, but the flurry of whispered speculation and rumour that followed her swift, unexpected marriage to Justin Thomas had not completely died down. It hung in the air like tiny, almost invisible eddies of dust, always present but only occasionally seen. 'How could she have married him?' people had murmured. 'Wasn't she engaged to his brother, Luke?' Once, working late in her office, Caitlin had overheard part of a conversation between two of the night-cleaning crew.

'This new boss of ours must be some cold broad,' a gruff male voice had said. 'She finds out that her boyfriend got killed in some jungle somewhere, so she just turns around and marries the guy's brother. And then, when Mr Thomas dropped dead, too, she didn't even miss a beat. Just moved into his office, cool as you please, and took over his job.'

'Yeah, well, that's what they call moving up the corporate ladder, George,' a second voice had chuckled. 'The lady had her eye on the top spot all along, I guess. Hell of a way to go about it, though.'

'If you were a good-looking broad, you'd do the same thing. What the hell, if you can hook the first brother, why not do the same to the second?'

The men had begun to laugh lewdly, and Caitlin had waited until their voices drifted away before hurrying from her office into the empty corridor. In the following months, she'd steadfastly refused to acknowledge the conversations that stopped when she got within earshot and the faces that turned away from her as she approached. Gradually, as time passed, scepticism had given way to respect. Thomas Pharmaceuticals had thrived, and her associates admitted she was a capable, resourceful businesswoman, although she knew they saw her as something of an enigma: a woman who was honest and fair to work for, efficient and capable in her field, but one who seemed to have no existence outside the redbrick walls of the company. It was only Jean who had begun to suspect that Catlin's dedication to corporate success was a disguise; now, uncharacteristically, she'd let the past slip into the present, talking about those long ago, almost forgotten dreams of Paris ... Caitlin sat up straighter and shook her head impatiently. At least, she assured herself, she hadn't mentioned Luke's name.

She stood and walked slowly to the window. Almost reluctantly, she pulled back the curtains and looked outside. Darkness covered the city like a velvet caress. There seemed to be lights shimmering everywhere, illuminating the buildings, the streets, the streams of cars passing below. Caitlin's eyes lifted and searched the skyline, until the looming figure of the Eiffel Tower, its delicate skeleton lit like an arrow soaring into the black sky, filled her vision. She thought of the times she and Luke had talked of climbing to the top of the tower.

'I don't think they let you,' she'd said solemnly.

'We'll manage something,' he'd teased. 'Remember, running up those steps will put us in shape for the Louvre.'

And she had laughed and nodded her head. 'I know, I know. We have to do it in record time. Seven minutes from the door to the Winged Victory . . .'

'Six,' he'd said quickly, tweaking her nose. 'Up the steps, to the Winged Victory, and around the Venus de Milo. We'll wear running shoes and fly past all the other tourists.'

Caitlin shuddered and bowed her head, resting it against the chilled window pane. After four years, she could still hear his voice, still see his slightly crooked grin, almost feel his arm around her.

'We'll make love in a field of poppies, Cat,' he'd promised in a husky whisper, holding her tightly in his arms.

Somehow, nothing seemed as real as those memories: not her success as director of the firm Luke and his brother had controlled, not even the terrible six months of her marriage to Justin. Reality was the past, the love she and Luke had shared, the plans they'd made together ... Caitlin drew in her breath. Reality, she reminded herself with cruel precision, was that Luke was dead. He had been taken from her forever. Only the corporation he'd loved and the ideals he'd died for remained, and she would go on doing whatever must be done to keep his dream alive. Decisively, she straightened her skirt, smoothed down her jacket, and flicked off the lights as she left the conference room.

Her suite was on a higher floor, and her glance flickered over the faces of couples waiting for the elevator. Jean was right, she thought unhappily. This was, indeed, a city for lovers. She looked away from their smiling faces, trying to ignore their whispered conversations and aura of pleased discovery. Briskly, she strode down the corridor, her room key dangling in her hand. The sitting room of the small suite was elegant, charmingly decorated with fine antiques, but tonight they failed to interest her. She walked to the window and pulled the curtains to block out the blazing view of the city that wrenched at her heart.

'Get to work, Caitlin,' she whispered to herself. 'What's the matter with you tonight?'

She dropped her briefcase on a table and hurried into the bedroom. In the dark, she pulled off her clothing, dropping it, with uncharacteristic lack of care, on the bed. She reached into the cupboard and searched for her robe. Finally, with a hiss of irritation, she switched on the bedside lamp. Caitlin stumbled backwards in disbelief. There, artfully arranged in a porcelain bowl, was a profusion of red poppies, their bright colour like a splash of blood against the white of the porcelain.

'Jean!' she said aloud, reaching for the phone. How foolish she'd been to mention the poppies to her secretary, she thought, as she dialled the front desk. Jean had meant well, but . . . A carefully neutral voice murmured, '*Bon soir.*'

'*Bon soir*,' Caitlin said, trying to keep the edge of annoyance she felt out of her voice. '*Voici Caitlin Thomas, et je voudrais* . . . Do you speak English?' she asked, somewhat impatiently.

'Yes, of course,' the impersonal voice answered testily. 'What is it you wish, Madame?'

'There are some flowers in my suite—some poppies. I'd like them removed at once, please.'

'I know nothing of flowers in your suite, Madame,' the voice countered immediately. 'If they are an annoyance to you, please put them outside the door, and I assure you, they will be removed.'

'I don't want them outside my door,' Caitlin said evenly. 'I don't want them anywhere near me, do you understand?' She took a deep breath and turned away from the poppies. 'Monsieur,' she said, more calmly and politely, 'I . . . I'm allergic to flowers. It's very important that these be taken away at once. Will you please see to it?'

There was the briefest of pauses. 'But of course, Madame,' the voice purred, its tone suggesting that this was yet another eccentric American tourist to be dealt with. 'The porter will be there at once.'

'Thank you . . . *merci beaucoup.*' Caitlin hung up the phone, carefully avoiding any contact with the flowers. Again, she reached into the cupboard, flipping past the dresses and suits hanging within it until she found her old flannel robe. Grateful for the feeling of comfort it gave her, she snuggled into it, tying the belt around her narrow waist just as she heard a discreet knock at the door. Quickly, she snatched up the poppies and hurried into the sitting room.

'Thank you for coming so quickly,' she said,

flinging open the door and thrusting the bowl out in front of her. Jean's bewildered face looked back at her. 'Jean?' Caitlin said in surprise. 'I, uh, I didn't expect ... umm, thank you for the poppies, but I prefer ... I'm allergic, you see, and ...' Her stammered words broke off and she blushed. 'It was very kind of you, I'm sure, but ...'

Jean grasped the porcelain bowl with both hands and gave Caitlin a questioning look. 'All offerings are gladly accepted,' she said lightly. 'But I didn't send them. And it's news for me that you're allergic, Caitlin. I'll have to stop putting those chrysanthemums in your office back home, huh?' Her eyes glinted mischievously.

Caitlin's blush deepened. 'I'm only allergic to certain kinds,' she said quickly. 'And if you didn't send these, who did?'

'Search me. Maybe they're a gift from the management, or from the Marquis. Anyway, I'll be glad to get rid of them for you. I know the perfect spot in my room for them.'

'Yes, well, enjoy them,' Caitlin said slowly. 'I guess they must be from the Marquis, although I can't imagine why he'd choose poppies.' She shook her head and forced herself to smile. 'Well,' she added briskly, 'what are you doing here? I thought you were off to explore Paris.'

Jean sighed with frustration. 'Would you believe it's raining out there? I figured I'd let you know I was back, just in case you needed me for anything.'

'Thanks, but I can handle the rest of the work on my own. I'm sorry your plans fizzled out.'

Her secretary chuckled. 'Drizzled out is more like it. I guess I'll turn on my television and brush up on my French. Anyway, if you need me, just call.'

'Oh, one thing—would you mind finding the hall

porter for me? He's supposed to come by and pick up these flowers. Just tell him I won't be needing him, okay?'

'Will do, Caitlin. Good night—and don't forget to eat something.'

'I won't, I promise. I'm going to call room service right now,' she added when Jean raised a disbelieving eyebrow.

Caitlin closed the door and leaned back against it. She'd have to phone the Marquis tomorrow and thank him, she supposed, although she'd have to find a nice way to tell him that poppies were the last flowers she ever wanted to see or touch again. Stifling a yawn, she started back to the bedroom when there was a knock at the door. The porter, she thought, retracing her steps. Jean must have missed him.

She drew the robe more tightly around her and opened the door. 'I'm sorry to have bothered you,' she began, and then the words caught in her throat, as if a hand had closed around her neck and choked off all sound and breath. She felt the blood draining from her face, heard the sudden, frightening thump of her heart as her eyes fought to focus on the figure standing in the doorway, even heard, as from a great distance, the faint sound of her own voice, somewhere between a moan and a cry, as her mind tried to accept what she saw before her.

'My God,' she gasped hoarsely, as the corridor and the figure began to merge into a swirling mass of confused image and colour, 'my God, Luke ... Luke ...'

The man in the doorway smiled sardonically. 'Hello, Cat,' he said, almost casually, leaning one hand against the door frame. 'Glad to see me?'

'You can't be ...' she said, the words a strangled whisper, as her hands reached out to touch him.

'You're ... I thought ... they said you were dead,' she gasped, as the room began to swim away from her.

'You shouldn't have been so quick to believe them, Cat,' he said, closing the door behind him. 'I told you I'd come back, remember? Aren't you going to kiss me hello?'

The last thing she remembered was the sound of his words, echoing over and over through the empty vortex her mind had become, as she slipped to the floor at his feet.

CHAPTER TWO

CAITLIN felt herself lifted in strong arms, held in a remembered embrace that was familiar yet somehow strangely impersonal. She was struggling back to the light, fighting out of the grey haze that had claimed her, when she was dropped, unceremoniously, on the couch. Gradually, the sensation of spinning in a formless void lessened, and her eyes fluttered open, focusing again on that face she'd never forgotten.

'Luke? Is it really you?' she murmured haltingly.

He was seated opposite her, legs crossed, an expression somewhere between amusement and annoyance on his handsome face. He nodded his head and leaned back in the chair.

'Nobody else,' he agreed. 'I figured you'd be surprised to see me.'

She sat up on the low-slung couch and stared at him. 'Surprised?' she repeated slowly, her eyes widening in disbelief. 'I'm ... I'm astounded ... I ... I'm ... there's no way to tell you ...' She ran her tongue over her lips, her eyes drinking in the sight of his lean, tanned face, his hazel eyes, his mouth. 'The poppies,' she whispered in a voice that barely seemed her own, they were from you, weren't they?' He nodded, the strange half-smile on his face. Suddenly, the full realisation of what was happening flooded over her, and she sprang from the couch and hurled herself against him, wrapping her arms tightly around his neck, burying her face against his chest. 'My love, my love,' she cried softly, all her senses filled with the wonder of this moment, 'you're here ... really here ... you're alive ...'

He drew in his breath and his hand touched her hair. Then, his body stiffened and his hand dropped to his side.

'Very much so, Cat,' he said in the cool, impersonal tones of a stranger. 'What was it Mark Twain said? "Rumours of my death have been greatly exaggerated", wasn't it? Well, that about sums it up.'

She waited for his arms to enfold her, for him to lift her from her knees as she knelt before him and raise her face to his. But he was immobile, his muscles tense and unyielding beneath her hands, and finally she drew back, her hands trailing across his chest as they fell from his neck.

'What is it, darling?' she asked softly, her eyes fixed on his. 'Are you ill?'

He pushed back his chair and walked to the window. 'I'm fine,' he said evenly. 'I'm alive and well.'

Slowly, never taking her eyes from him, she rose to her feet. 'It's a miracle,' she whispered. 'They said you'd been killed—that guerrillas shelled the truck you were travelling in—that there were four of you inside it, and all of you were . . . were . . .'

'You've got all the details right,' he said, leaning back against the wall. 'Except for one, Cat. I didn't die.'

'Thank God for that,' she said softly. 'But I don't understand what happened. It's been so long—almost four years . . .'

'Three years and eight months in beautiful Central America,' he said with heavy sarcasm. 'I can even tell you how many days, if you like. The minutes and seconds are a little more difficult, of course, but with a little effort, I can figure that out, too.'

It took a few seconds for his words to make sense to her. All the while he was speaking, her eyes kept sweeping over him, drinking in the sight of him, as she struggled to accept that this man who stood before her was real, not some long-dreamed-of apparition conjured from the depths of her own loneliness. Finally, she moistened her lips and moved slowly towards him.

'You mean you were captured?' she whispered incredulously. 'You've been a prisoner all this time?'

His lips drew back from his teeth in a terrible parody of a smile. 'Yes, that's exactly what I mean. Quite a surprise, isn't it?'

'A surprise?' she repeated, her voice trembling. 'It's wonderful ... it's ...' She reached out to touch him and he moved away from her.

'Don't you want to hear the whole story, Caitlin? After all, it's not every day a dead man turns up on your doorstep.'

A sharp, stabbing pain knifed through her. What dreadful things had happened to him, she wondered, staring at the face she knew so well, noticing the terrible weariness in his eyes and the furrows beside his mouth. And why was he talking to her in this cold, distant way? She longed to hold him and comfort him, but he had put a distance between them that she was afraid to cross. Stories about Vietnam raced through her mind, along with accounts she'd read of the psychological trauma suffered by hostages and captives, and she forced herself to remain calm, to hold back the emotions raging through her.

'Of course I want to hear it, Luke. But ...' She broke off in mid-sentence as he turned towards the light and she saw a narrow, jagged line high across one cheek, running up into his eyebrow. With a muffled cry, she leaned forward and touched the scar with her fingertip. 'You've been hurt,' she cried. 'Oh, Luke ...'

He flinched as if her light touch had scalded him. 'It's nothing, Cat. Just a souvenir of my trip, you might say. Not as pleasant as a roll of film or a postcard, but that's all it is.'

She shook her head and again her hand lifted towards his face. 'But how did it happen?'

'Don't worry about it,' he said sharply. He moved away before she could touch him and sat in the chair again. 'Why don't you just let me tell about beautiful, exotic Central America, Cat? I'll bet you never heard a travelogue quite like this one.'

She sat down opposite him and waited. He reached into his pocket and pulled out a pack of cigarettes and she wondered, fleetingly, when he had started to smoke. His hand trembled slightly as he lit up and she bit her lip, remembering how strong and steady those hands had been when he worked with the delicate equipment in his laboratory, how sure and assertive their touch when he'd caressed her.

'I want to hear everything,' she said softly. 'But not now. It's enough that you're here.'

'We do have to talk about it,' he said quickly, tossing the cigarette pack aside. 'I've been waiting for this chance for days.'

'Then tell me,' she murmured.

'Remember I said I might have to end up dragging those drugs up a mountainside on a donkey if they were ever going to get where they were really needed? Well, I was damned close to being right. It took me about half a day to figure out that none of the prior shipments had reached the people who needed them because the government was as corrupt as the guerrillas said it was.' He paused and took a deep breath, his eyes following the trail of white smoke from the cigarette as if there were images trapped in it that only he could see. 'So I talked to some people, checked around a little, and I hooked up with three other guys who wanted to get out of the city and up into the hills.'

He grinned wolfishly and stubbed out his cigarette. 'Yeah, those were my buddies. A guy from some peace group, a medical missionary, and a hot-shot reporter from some little paper nobody every heard of. We crammed ourselves into this old truck full of food and medicine and set out to save the world.' He laughed bitterly and leaned back in the chair. 'Only, it didn't quite work out that way.'

That would be just like him, she thought, putting his ideals and hopes before any concern for himself. That was the Luke she knew and loved, the Luke who would have wrapped her in his arms the second she opened the door. She forced back a tremor of apprehension and concentrated on his words.

'We were so careful, we thought, so cautious. We left the city at night. By daybreak, we were in the mountains.'

'But if you were careful ... Where were you going? There was fighting in the mountains; all the newspapers said so ...'

He got to his feet and stalked across the room. 'A guy from UNESCO told us there was a village up there. Just women and kids, he said, starving, dying, cut off from everything.' He swung around and faced her again. 'We were almost there. At least, that's what we thought. It was just about noon; I remember that the sun was like a white-hot ball, high overhead, and one of the guys, the reporter, I think, had just said he'd give anything for the sight of a hamburger stand, and we were laughing at that, when ... when they opened fire on us.'

Caitlin leaned forward, her hands tightly clasped in her lap. 'The guerrillas?'

'How the hell should I know?' he growled. 'Maybe ... probably. There were so many factions you needed a computer to keep track of them all. Whoever they were, they hit us with everything they had. The next thing I knew, the truck was on its side in a gully and they were all dead. The three guys with me—wiped out, gone. I was the only one left, and there wasn't a scratch on me.'

She let out her breath in a long sigh. 'Thank God,' she whispered. 'I'm sorry for the others, but at least you ... But then how ... they said they'd ... they'd identified your remains, Luke. They said there'd been a fire but the government sent us your watch, your ring ...'

'You underestimate me, Cat,' he said curtly. 'Remember, before I left, we talked about some guy who'd been kidnapped in El Salvador and held for ransom? I figured that's what they'd do with me. So I dumped my watch and ring on what was left of the guy from the peace group,' he said, a shudder passing through him, 'and I took his identification. I'd made it to the other side of the gully when the truck exploded and became an inferno. Nothing was left. Luke Thomas just ceased to exist. That's when they captured me.'

The rush of words stopped and silence held them in its webbed embrace. Finally, Caitlin stood up and walked to his side.

'But what happened? That was four years ago ...'

'Three years and eight months, Cat,' he said swiftly. 'For a long time, they argued about what to do with me, trying to figure out a way to get some money for me, I suppose. But the guy whose papers I'd taken was a peace groupie; nobody had ever heard of him and nobody looked for him. After a while, I guess I just started to blend into the background. Oh, they'd trot me out to score points when they wanted to impress somebody, but they got a little sloppy guarding me twenty-four hours a day, so a couple of weeks ago, I decided to take my chances. I slipped away one night and here I am.'

'And you've come home,' Caitlin whispered. His laugh cut through the room like the sound of shattering glass, and she forced herself to smile tremulously. 'Well, I know this isn't home, but I meant ... you've come back to me, Luke. I used to pray it might happen, that your death had been a bad dream ...'

He laughed again and tears welled in her eyes at the ugly sound of it.

'That's good, Cat, really good. What a picture it conjures up: you, sitting by the fireside back home, crying for your lost love, hoping for his return.' Suddenly, he stepped closer to her and his hand clamped around her wrist. 'But that's not quite the way it was, Cat, isn't that right?'

'That's just the way it was,' she said quickly, wincing at the pressure on her wrist. 'For days, for weeks, I couldn't bring myself to believe that you'd died.' The tears she'd been fighting spilled from her eyes and coursed down her cheeks as all her self-control vanished. 'And now you're here—you're alive—and I don't understand what's going on,' she sobbed. 'What's wrong? Why are you so ... so angry? This should be the most wonderful moment in our lives.'

'Cut it out, Caitlin,' he growled. 'I told you what I've been doing for the past four years; now I want to hear your story, starting with the week after you got the news of my death.'

His fingers bit into her wrist one last time and then he flung her hand aside.

'Oh, God,' she whispered, her face whitening as she

'saw the truth of what he believed reflected in his eyes. You know about Justin . . .'

'It's so much easier when the dead stay buried, isn't it, Cat?' His words were barely audible, a serpentine hiss filled with malice. 'When there's no one to answer to, or to spoil all your carefully made plans.'

'Luke, please,' she said desperately, 'you must listen to me. You don't understand . . .'

'Oh, but I do, sweet sister-in-law. I've had all the last week to get it figured out.' His mouth twisted in a bitter smile and his eyes darkened. 'It took me days to get down the damned mountain, through miles of wild country and safely back to the city. When I finally turned up at the home of the American Consul, I must have looked like a creature from another planet, but he knew me. He couldn't believe it; he wanted to know everything—where I'd been, how I'd survived—but all I wanted to do was talk to you and Justin.' His breathing quickened and his voice dropped to an icy whisper. 'So I placed a call to San José, to the office, and I asked to speak with Justin Thomas. I didn't ask for you, dear Caitlin,' he said, warping those words with a cruel irony that made her shudder, 'because I was afraid hearing my voice would be too great a shock for you.'

Caitlin closed her eyes, knowing what he would say next, imagining how he must have staggered under the blow.

'I asked to speak with Justin Thomas,' he whispered, moving closer to her as if to share some terrible secret, 'and the receptionist said I must mean Mrs Thomas. I didn't know what the hell she was talking about, and I said no, it was Mr Thomas I wanted, and she gave this uncomfortable little laugh, said I was really out of touch with things, that Justin had been dead for three years.

'Then she dropped the other shoe, Cat,' he continued softly, his eyes burning into hers. 'When I didn't say anything—couldn't say anything, really—she asked if I was still on the line. I finally managed to say that I was, and I guess I asked for you then. That's how I found out you'd become Mrs Justin Thomas, the executive director of Thomas Pharmaceuticals. She kept asking me who I was, and I finally managed to say I was just an old friend, that my name wasn't important. I don't even remember hanging up the phone; all I recall is feeling as if something had hit me in the gut.'

Silence enveloped them, broken only by the harsh sound of his breathing. Frantically, Caitlin searched for a way to explain everything to him without adding to his pain, until at last she took a deep breath and tried to still the trembling of her body.

'Luke,' she said carefully, choosing each word with precision, 'I know how you must feel. Let me explain . . .'

'Don't bother,' he said abruptly. 'My attorney already did. The next call I made was to him. Jack brought me up to date, Cat. I know all about the charming funeral service you and Thomas Pharmaceuticals arranged for me, and all about your wedding to Justin a few days later.' Again, that terrible smile lit his face. 'Thank you for that. It was gracious of you to have at least done things in that order.'

'I know how it must look to you,' she said quickly, reaching out towards him. 'I know it looks bad . . .'

'Bad?' he repeated incredulously, his voice rising. 'It looks tawdry. That's a better word, don't you think? It looks cheap. It looks grasping. It looks precisely like what it is.'

Each word struck at her like a slap in the face, and

she felt the colour rising to her cheeks, but she stood her ground without flinching as the ugly accusations fell from his lips.

'You know you don't mean that, Luke,' she said quietly. 'I know you're hurt and upset, but you know me better than to think those things of me. If you'd just listen to me, you'd understand.'

'What don't I understand, Cat? That you saw your chance and took it? That you grieved about as long for me as you did for Justin? That you went from my distraught fiancée to my brother's wife to head of the corporation in, what was it, Cat, six months? You must be proud of yourself; that's a lot of progress to have made in so short a time.'

Hesitantly, her hand touched his arm, as if by bridging the physical gap between them she might reach beyond this hollow-eyed, cold-voiced stranger and find the man she loved.

'You're tired,' she murmured, 'and under a lot of stress. Anyone would be, coming back to all this after years of being held prisoner. I guess all of this looks bad ... I guess it might appear bad to others, but ...'

Angrily, he shrugged away from her hand.

'I've been a prisoner in Central America, Cat, not an inmate in an institution. Stop placating me and start dealing in the truth, or is that impossible for you?'

'All right,' she said quickly, determined not to antagonise him any further, fighting to find a way to get through to him. 'I know how it looked. But I didn't care what others thought, Luke. You're the only one who can understand why I had to do what I did.'

'What's that supposed to mean?' he demanded. 'You married Justin, didn't you? You control the company, don't you?'

'Yes, yes, but there was a reason for what I did. It began . . . it began when we heard you were dead,' she said slowly, even now shuddering at the sound of those words. 'I wanted to die, too. There was suddenly nothing left to live for; my life had ended before it began. That truck exploded and burned in my thoughts a thousand times, and I died along with you each time it happened.'

He crossed over to the couch and sat down on it, his eyes sweeping over her as she stood alone in the centre of the room, her cheeks damp with tears, her arms wrapped around herself as if for warmth, and he smiled unpleasantly.

'That's really touching. Let me be sure I've got this straight. You suffered terribly when you heard I was dead, you wanted to die, too, and then, after the smoke cleared, after a couple of days had gone by, you looked around and there was Justin.'

'No,' she said sharply, raising her head and staring at him angrily. 'That's not the way it was at all. You said you wanted the truth, so listen to it.'

'What I want to hear is how you got my brother to marry you, Cat. He didn't even like you, for God's sake.'

'You don't know the first thing about how Justin felt about me,' she said stiffly.

He threw back his head and laughed. 'Oh, how wrong you are, sweet sister-in-law. I know all too well he thought you weren't to be trusted, the way you were always flirting with him behind my back.'

Caitlin drew in her breath and colour flamed in her face. 'What?' she gasped. 'That's a lie, Luke. I never looked at Justin, or anybody else, from the time I graduated from college and went to work at Thomas's. You know that.'

He shrugged his shoulders and pulled a cigarette from the crumpled pack that lay on the coffee table.

'But it looks as if I was wrong. After all, you seduced him into a marriage proposal, didn't you?'

She moved across the room towards him, fists clenched at her sides, trying to control the anger rising within her reminding herself that this man—this stranger before her—was the man she'd loved and sacrificed for, that he had been though a living hell the past four years, that he was probably still under greater stress than she could imagine. Carefully, as if she were picking her way through fragments of broken glass, she collected her thoughts before she spoke.

'He asked me to marry him,' she said slowly. 'And I had to, because of the corporation . . .'

'At last,' Luke snapped. 'The truth comes out. You wanted the corporation, and you finally got it. I was gone, and Justin was your last chance.'

'Do you know what you're saying?' she demanded. 'Do you hear yourself? I don't care what you've been through. You can't really believe that.'

'Justin knew the truth about you, Cat. He knew you wanted to do more than putter around the office, supervising the staff, keeping our books.'

She stared at him in disbelief. 'That's insane—insane! I loved my job.'

'A woman like you,' he continued, his voice rising over hers, 'with a degree in business administration, with job offers from big corporations, happy in a job like that? Wasting your time in a place where you couldn't move up, go to the top, because Justin and I already held those spots. It didn't make sense. Justin tried to make me see it, but I was just too blind to face facts.'

'What facts?' she demanded angrily. 'The only fact was that I loved you, that I believed in Thomas's the way you did, that I was happy to be there, working with you, ever since you gave me my first summer job.'

'The truth, dear Caitlin, was that you thought your father should have got more than a five percent share for his work, and you were determined to get your hands on everything you thought was rightfully yours.'

Her head snapped back as if he'd struck her. 'Those are Justin's words,' she said hoarsely, 'not yours. Why would you even have listened to him? After all we meant to each other, all our plans ... We never doubted each other, Luke,' she added desperately, her eyes and voice pleading with him to remember. 'That last day we spent together, on the beach—have you forgotten the things we promised, how we almost ... how hard it was for us to let go of each other?'

He fumbled the last cigarette from the pack and lit it, inhaling deeply before he answered.

'He warned me about that, too,' he finally said, his voice cool and remote. 'You really had me going, Cat. All that heavy breathing, those stolen moments on the beach at Big Sur.' He smiled at the blush that spread over her cheeks. 'That innocent blush you still do so well. And all those whispers, all those promises.'

The silence between them lengthened until seconds seemed like hours. There seemed no way to answer him, no way to choose between the anger and despair churning within her, and finally Caitlin backed away from him.

'I don't know you,' she murmured. 'You're not the man I loved. You're someone else, someone cruel and hateful.' Choking back the rest of the words that she might say, she turned away from him. 'Please,' she said quickly, 'leave now, Luke. Leave before we have nothing left. You need some rest, or maybe you need a doctor ... I keep telling myself to remember all you've been through, but there's a limit ...'

'You watch too many soap operas, Cat,' he said

evenly. 'These four years were bad, but not as bad as you imagine. Oh, things were pretty rough at first, but then they began to ease off. And once Maria came on the scene . . . He smiled slightly and shrugged. 'Well, Maria didn't hate this gringo the way the others did.'

'Maria?' she repeated tonelessly. 'Who was Maria?'

He got to his feet. 'What's the difference? Let's just say our relationship was one of the reasons I managed to survive. Relationships are strange things, aren't they, Cat?' he added, walking towards her. 'I mean, just look at how things were between Justin and me. We disagreed a lot, but we managed to keep a kind of peace between us just because we were brothers. The one thing that almost finished us was you.'

Caitlin nodded her head. 'I see,' she said evenly. 'Now you're going to blame me for the trouble between the two of you.'

'I said you were the thing that *almost* finished us. He kept on telling me you were wrong for me, you see, making accusations, and I kept on insisting he was wrong, that he didn't really know you.' He took a deep breath and ran his hand through his hair. 'God, it's a hell of thing to find out, after all these years, after he's dead and gone, that he was right.'

This can't be happening, Caitlin thought suddenly. This must be a dream, a nightmare. Any second now, my alarm clock will go off and I'll wake up in bed, clutching at the tangled sheets, safe in my own apartment back in San José . . . But Luke's voice was all too real, echoing through the elegant sitting room, reverberating through her head, until at last she slapped her hands over her hears and shook her head from side to side.

'Stop it,' she demanded. 'Don't say any more, I beg you.'

'Why? What does it matter now, Cat?'

'You're killing everything, Luke. Everything.'

He moved towards her as silently and swiftly as a serpent. 'You killed it, Caitlin,' he said roughly. 'I should have listed to Justin. He was right about you from the start. Do you know what he called you? A professional virgin! A woman scrambling for the top, for sale to the highest bidder, ready to cash in on her most valuable asset. I guess it didn't matter to you which brother you snared, just so long as you got one of us. It just amazes me that Justin tumbled into your trap, but I suppose it only proves you're really good at what you do. You must be pleased with yourself.'

Like a tautly strung bow under pressure it was never designed to withstand, Caitlin's rage snapped free of the restraints she'd tried so hard to maintain. There was nothing left within her but the all-consuming need to hurt him as he had hurt her, to wipe that cold, steely look from his face and make him suffer. Her head sprang up so that her eyes met his squarely, and she stepped forward until no space remained between them.

'Pleased with myself?' she hissed. 'You can't imagine how inadequate a description that is. I had the good sense to marry the right brother, you see.' His face was an unchanging mask and she plunged wildly ahead, searching blindly for the words that would pierce him and draw blood. 'But you're wrong about one thing; it did matter to me which brother I married. I wanted the stronger one, the dominant one, and that's the one I got.' Something in his eyes darkened, changed substance, and she gathered herself for the final thrust. 'And I'm glad I was a virgin. At least, when I gave myself to someone, it was to a real man, one who knew what he wanted and wasted no time in taking it. Justin was twice the man you ever were. Maybe we only had a few months together, but they were months I'll never forget.'

The room seemed filled with the sound of her ragged breathing. She was trembling from head to toe, shaken as much by her desperate, terrible lies as by all he had said to her. She watched his face, hoping even now for some reaction from him, some faint glimmer of the man she'd known and loved, but he said nothing. Finally, exhausted and spent, she turned away and started for the door, wanting nothing so much as to be free of the sight of him.

'We have nothing more to say to each other, Luke, so I'd appreciate it if you'd just . . .'

Suddenly, he grasped her by the shoulders and spun her around to face him.

'Not just yet,' he said softly, his voice weighted with malice. 'Four years ago, I thought my problem was going to be living long enough to escape from that village. Now, my problem is you. You have what's mine, Cat. I came here tonight to warn you, although it's more than you deserve. You see, I know about next week's meeting. That's why I'm here, because I have my own agenda to pursue.'

'You have no shares to vote,' she said coldly. 'You won't be there.'

'I don't have to attend a meeting to tell my family what a witch you really are, Cat. By the time I get finished, they'll fall over themselves for the chance to get rid of you. And then, after they've voted you out of your fancy job, I'll start legal action against you and get back my stock in Thomas's, mine and Justin's. I owe him that much, at least.'

Everything had come full circle, Caitlin thought wildly. The corporate shares that had started all this, that had brought them to this fateful moment, were the only reason he had come to Paris. She could end it all now with a simple gesture . . .

'If the stock is what you want,' she said calmly, 'you

could have simply asked me for it. Did that ever occur to you?'

Luke's lips drew back from his teeth. 'You must take me for a fool, Cat. No, my dear Mrs Thomas, my sweet sister-in-law, I'm going to get what belongs to me, and I'll be damned if I'll give you the chance to play any more games with me.'

The last regrets for the lies she'd told him, for whatever he had endured, vanished in a burst of anger that flushed her face with crimson heat.

'Then be damned, Luke Thomas,' she cried as she wrenched open the door. 'And you'd better dig in for a long, hard fight, because that's precisely what it's going to be.'

CHAPTER THREE

CAITLIN sat huddled in the darkness of the night, hiding in the surrounding silence, trying to make herself one with the sombre shadows in her room. Her eyes felt swollen and gritty with tears, and her cheeks were damp from their passage. She glanced at the small, enamelled clock on the bedside table; it was past two in the morning, hours since she'd slammed the door after Luke, hours since she'd given up any hope of sleep. She rose and paced impatiently from one wall to the other, but the suite seemed to hold her prisoner to her own thoughts, as her mind played and replayed the accusations Luke had hurled at her and the damning lies with which she'd responded.

Hurriedly, she took off her robe and scrambled into a pair of slacks and a sweater. Grabbing her raincoat, she fled, walking quickly through the empty hotel corridor, clattering down the back stairs. Within minutes, she was standing on the broad Avenue George V, her collar turned up high around her neck, her hands plunged deep into her pockets, barely noticing the few late-night strollers who glanced at her huddled form with curiosity.

She walked without direction or purpose, and when finally she saw the Seine ahead of her, the lights along the river like jewelled beacons in the mist, she hesitated only briefly before walking down the steps leading to the promenade beside the water. It was too late for the Bateaux-Mouches to be running; the darkened shapes of the sightseeing boats were huddled against the bank like a great herd of prehistoric beasts, gathered together for the night. A pair of lovers embraced in the shadows; Caitlin hurried past them, eyes downcast, trying to ignore the memories their joined silhouettes ignited. At last, her steps slowed, and she sighed wearily and sat down on a bench facing the black water. She watched the reflections of the lights along the river as they danced on the gentle undulations of the Seine, fighting against the despair and exhaustion that threatened to overwhelm her, until, suddenly, she bowed her head and hot tears filled her eyes again.

'Luke,' she whispered into the cool damp night, 'Luke...' Her cry faded, unanswered, into the mist.

Life was nothing but a game of chance, she thought, a game determined by the toss of the dice on some great, cosmic table. There was no other way to explain the cruel joke fate had played tonight. Luke had come back, miraculously returned to her, and yet his only purpose was to destroy her. Reality and fantasy had merged to create a nightmare. The anger that had sheltered and protected her hours before was gone, driven back by a pain that was almost beyond endurance. Deprived of his love, she felt fragile and empty. Only her love for him, her belief in what they had meant to each other, had nourished her from the second she'd learned of his death.

'What are you going to do, Caitlin?' Justin had demanded the day after the news had arrived. 'Fade away and die, too, like a heroine in a Victorian tragedy? You're far too tough to do that, I hope.'

She'd raised her head and looked at Justin in disbelief. 'He was your brother, for God's sake. Don't you feel anything? How can you accept his death so easily?'

A scowl had creased his dark face, so unlike Luke's it had almost been impossible to recognise the two men as brothers.

'Of course I feel something, Caitlin. Luke was my younger brother; we worked together every day since our parents died.' The scowl had deepened and he had shrugged his shoulders. 'At least they had the good sense to lose their lives in a plane crash while they were on vacation, instead of dying in some bug-infested jungle for no good reason.'

'What a stupid, cruel thing to say,' she had blazed angrily, the colour rising to her pale face. 'Death is never sensible, Justin. Luke didn't plan to have this happen; he wanted that shipment of drugs to get through to the people that needed them, and he was convinced it would if he delivered it himself.' Suddenly, her eyes filled with tears and she buried her face in her hands. 'I begged him not to go,' she had sobbed. 'You should have stopped him,' she had said angrily, raising her tear-streaked face to his. 'Why didn't you?'

Justin had smiled coldly. 'My dear brother was always such an idealist, Caitlin. He wouldn't have listened to me. My ideas didn't count for much where Luke was concerned, did they?'

'That isn't true,' she had answered quickly. 'Just look at this place,' she had added, gesturing at the office in which they sat. 'You worked together to build Thomas Pharmaceuticals into a respected company.'

'Which is precisely what it was when our father died,' Justin had said flatly. 'I wanted to expand into cosmetics and toiletries, but Luke . . '

'I don't want to argue with you, Justin. Not when we've only just learned that he's . . . he's . . .' A sob had caught in Caitlin's throat and she had bowed her head. 'If only he'd let someone else make that delivery.'

Justin's hollow laughter had reverberated throughout the office. 'And let someone else share in the glory?' he had growled, shaking his head. 'Not very likely, my dear. Baby brother was bound and determined to be a hero. He was going to get that shipment through, come hell or high water.'

Caitlin's eyes had darkened with anger, but her voice had remained low and controlled. 'He wasn't trying to be heroic. He just wanted to do what was right.'

'What was right?' he had repeated sarcastically, staring at her with a half-smile on his face. 'You always said that about Luke. When he insisted profits were high enough on our regular products so we could keep mark-ups low on some of the new drugs we shipped abroad, you said he was doing the right thing. When he argued against dropping production levels so we could claim a higher price for the vaccine we developed last year, you backed him.' His mouth had twisted with anger and he had leaned closer to her, until she could see nothing but his dark, brooding face. 'And you voted with your shares along with him, against me . . .'

'Justin . . .'

'Against me,' he had said steadily, his words clipped and precise, 'while my dear brother charmed the rest of the family into voting the same way. Was that the "right thing", Caitlin? Just tell me that. I was the one in charge of those decisions, not Luke. He was head of research and development. Why did he interfere in things that were none of his concern?'

'Justin, please. This isn't the time . . .'

'Damn it, Caitlin,' he had roared, slamming his hand down on the desk, 'this is exactly the time. Luke is dead. Dead, Caitlin. He's not here to get in the way of business any more.'

Caitlin had stared at him as he swayed above her. Until this moment, his angry ranting had seemed an outpouring of jealousy and bitterness. Now, a new note had crept into his voice, one that filled her with wrenching disgust.

'You almost sound as if you're glad he's ... he's dead,' she had finally whispered. 'But not even you could be that heartless.'

'I'm not heartless, Caitlin, merely realistic. It's time we dealt in truth, not ideals, and one of those truths is that my brother was blind to what this company is worth in dollars and cents. He wouldn't even listen to me when I wanted to sell out to Clarke Drugs a year ago. That offer they made us was worth millions, Caitlin. But at the stockholders' meeting, between your fancy-spread sheets and Luke's talk of "family", you convinced the others to vote me down.'

'That's just the point, Justin,' Caitlin had said wearily, leaning her head back and closing her eyes. 'Thomas has always been a family business, and Luke wanted to keep it that way, just as your father did. And all my figures proved is that it's been making lots of money, more than enough, for everybody.'

'There's no such thing as "enough" when it comes to money, Caitlin. Didn't your degree in business administration teach you that?'

She had shaken her head as if to clear it and had got to her feet. 'I can't believe we're talking this way,' she had said slowly, leaning on the desk for support. 'Luke is dead, and all you can think of is money. What kind of man are you?'

Justin's smile had made a chill run up her spine. 'The kind who wants to get on with life, Caitlin. If you want to wring your hands over my brother forever, I'm sorry for you. But I'm going to do what I believe in for the first time in years.'

She had drawn herself erect and stared at him, her green eyes like a cold blaze of fire in her pale face. 'What does that mean?' she had asked carefully.

'It means, my dear, that you'd better get our books and papers up to date. I'm going to contact Clarke Drugs and tell them I'm ready to sell as soon as Luke's will is probated.'

'No,' she had said quickly, her fists clenching by her sides, 'you don't mean that.'

He had smiled almost pleasantly and nodded his head. 'I mean every word of it, Caitlin.'

'But this company belonged to your father—to you, to Luke ...'

'And now it will belong to Clarke. You'll come out ahead, Caitlin. Your five percent will be worth ...'

'I know what it will be worth,' she had interrupted angrily. 'But I don't want it. Luke believed in Thomas. He wanted the name to go on forever, its research to continue ...'

'What my brother wanted doesn't cut any ice any more,' he had said bluntly. 'Anyway, wasn't it only a few months ago that you tried to persuade him to find out if Clarke was still interested? Don't tell me his death wiped all that good sense out of your lovely head.'

Caitlin's face had flushed with anger. 'If you eavesdropped on us,' she had said evenly, 'then you must also know that I only wanted Luke to be free of you, of your greed. I wanted him to start a new company, one he could run without you, but he was determined to make peace with you and to keep the company in the family, the way it's always been.'

She had flinched at the harsh sound of his laughter.

'I hate to shatter your illusions about the family, my dear, but they'll want to sell as badly as I do, now that Luke can't charm them away from my position any more. When they understand what kind of money is involved ...'

'You have all the money you could possibly want,'

she had said wildly, her voice rising. 'I keep track of all the accounts here, remember? You have almost a six-figure income, Justin, counting expenses and stock profits . . .'

'The sale to Clarke will make that look puny, Caitlin.'

She had stared at his smug face, her eyes wide with disbelief. Like a mouse scurrying for safety from the ominous shadow of a soaring hawk, she had searched for the words that would persuade him to discard his plan to disband the company that Luke had struggled to develop, to find a way to keep this one remaining remembrance of him alive.

'But they'll drop the vaccine research, or at least change it,' she had said at last. 'You know it doesn't always clear a profit from year to year. And they'll never maintain our policy on holding down prices on some of the drugs we ship to underdeveloped nations. And this,' she had gone on in a breathless rush, walking across the office and waving her arms, 'will just become a profit-and-loss statement to some gigantic, faceless corporation. And for what, Justin? Luke earned the same money you did; it was enough for him. It's enough for anybody, it's . . .'

'It's not enough for me,' he had said flatly, 'and that's the end of the discussion.'

Caitlin had fought back the wild desire to fly across the room and strike him, to wipe the confident, self-satisfied look from his face.

'I'll stop you,' she had said. 'I'll vote against you and I'll convince the others. I'll tell them . . .'

He had thrown back his head and laughed. 'Tell them what, my dear? That I'm just liable to make them fortunes overnight? That should really upset them, Caitlin, especially Aunt Emily. Her votes, combined with mine and Luke's, are all I need.' His smile had broadened into a lupine sneer. 'And, in case you're counting on swaying them with sentiment, I'm sure they'll be all the more eager to sell when I remind them that it was one of those "underdeveloped" nations that took Luke's life. I suspect some of my family will be only too happy to cloak their appetite for profit in moral indignation.' The smile had faded from his face and his eyes had narrowed to pinpoints of light. 'I want all our books ready for inspection by Clarke's accountants next week, Caitlin. Do you understand?'

'I understand, all right,' she had answered quickly, her voice trembling with rage and disgust. 'You're despicable. I should have told Luke the truth about you long ago, the things you said about him behind his back, how often you tried . . . you tried to paw me.'

He had grinned and a shudder had run through her. 'But you didn't, did you? I never did figure that out. I couldn't quite decide whether you kept quiet because you were afraid he wouldn't believe you, or because you didn't want to do anything to upset the great family moralist.'

'The answer is much simpler than that, Justin, but I doubt if it's one you could understand. I just didn't want to make trouble between the two of you.'

'Such a noble sentiment, but a bit misplaced, don't you think? You've been working here, managing this office, since your graduation from college. And you spent how many summers working here while you were in school? Three? Four? Come now, Caitlin. You know that there was always trouble, as you so delicately put it, between Luke and me. He was the one with the family's support, the one reporters always wanted to interview whenever we turned out some new drug, always the one . . .' Justin had taken a deep breath and jammed his shaking hands into his pockets. 'The "trouble",' he said, deliberately exaggerating the very sound of the word, 'between us was of his own making.'

Anger had blossomed within her like an iridescent flower as she looked at Justin's reddened face. She had thought of the years when her father had headed the laboratory and the innumerable times he'd told her about Justin's insistent attempts to exploit the company and about his ugly, unfounded jealousy of Luke, until it was hard to believe they were brothers. She wondered if Justin had ever understood the principle upon which his father had founded Thomas. Certainly, he'd never shared them. A dozen biting, stinging answers had sprung to her mind and just as suddenly dissipated. What good was it when all that mattered was that her love was dead?

'What are we doing?' she had whispered brokenly. 'Luke is dead, Justin. He was all I ever wanted...'

'He was all anybody ever wanted,' Justin had said savagely. 'I was the older brother, but I walked in his shadow for years. My mother's face used to light up when he came into the room. And my father—I know damn well that he would have left all his stock to Luke if he could have done it without feeling guilty.' His hand had slammed down on a pile of papers stacked on the desk and they had scattered across the floor like dry leaves before the wind. 'Well, it's over. They're gone, and now Luke is, too. And I'm going to dump this ... this ghost-filled place once and for all.'

In the sudden silence, the sound of his ragged, heavy breathing had seemed to fill the space between them. Caitlin had looked into his face as if seeing him clearly for the first time, almost overwhelmed as she glimpsed the twisted darkness of his mind.

'How pathetic,' she had whispered finally, her voice a faint, papery rustle in the stillness. 'You would destroy all this just to get even? To pay back old jealousies?'

Justin had shrugged and turned away from her. 'If it makes you feel better to see it that way . . .'

'But you can't do this,' Caitlin had insisted. 'Luke worked so hard to develop the research programme, to see that our drugs went where they were most needed . . . That's what he lived for. For God's sake, Justin, that's what he died for.'

He had spun around and faced her, a crafty smile on his face.

'Oh, he lived for more than that, my dear. Don't be so immodest. I stumbled across the two of you in dark corners any number of times, didn't I?'

She had stared at him disbelief. 'We were in love, Justin. We never tried to hide it. If you think I'm going to let you pervert what we felt for each other into something sordid . . .' She had taken a deep breath, fighting to maintain control of herself.

'It's so much easier not to be bound by scruples,' he had interrupted smoothly. 'I tried to come between the two of you for a long time, Caitlin. In fact, right up until the day he left for Central America, I made an effort to convince Luke that you were the wrong woman for him.'

Caitlin had pushed the hair back from her face with a trembling hand.

'Why would you want to drive us apart?'

'Lots of reasons,' he had answered casually. 'One dedicated idealist snapping at my heels was enough. I didn't need you around, too, always telling him he was right.' His dark eyes had raked over her and an angry, embarrassed flush had swept across her cheeks. 'I don't think Luke ever truly knew how to make the most of such a beautiful woman,' he had chuckled, grinning at her. 'I always suspected my brother carried idealism a bit too far. He never really gave you what you needed, did he, Caitlin?'

'How dare you?' she had whispered.

He had laughed softly and walked towards her. 'You haven't answered my question,' he had said, taking her by the shoulders.

She had raised her chin and stared at him. 'Let go of me,' she had said coldly. 'Or are you determined to prove you really are an animal, Justin?'

His hands had lingered on her for a second, and then he had smiled and let go of her. 'There's time for that,' he had said easily. 'After I tie up loose ends here, sell the business to Clarke . . .'

'I'm not going to let you do it,' Caitlin had said warningly. 'I promise you, I'll find a way to stop you, for Luke's sake.'

Justin had picked up a glass paperweight and turned it idly in his hands, watching as it reflected the late afternoon sunlight streaming through the windows. 'I see,' he had said carefully. 'Tell me, Caitlin, what would you do if you could do anything you liked with this company?'

'I'd go on with Luke's policies, continue the research funds. And I'd set up a fellowship in his name, endow a scholarship at a university.'

Justin had smiled and put the paperweight back on the desk. 'Such noble ideas, dear Caitlin. My brother would be proud of you. But I'm afraid they're going to remain only ideas. They don't quite mesh with my plans.'

'I told you, Justin, I'll find a way to stop you.'

'There is a way,' he had said, his face whitening. 'Would you care to hear it?'

She had stared at him with curiosity. There was something tense and frightening in his voice, a hint of something ominous in his expression. 'What way?' she had asked hesitantly.

'Marry me,' he had said quickly. 'If you do, I'll ...'

A burst of hyserical laughter had erupted from her throat. 'Marry you?' she had gasped, trying to catch her breath. 'My God, who's behaving like a character in a Victorian novel now? I just wish you had a moustache, Justin, so that you could twirl it while I wring my hands in distress.' She had wiped her eyes with the back of her hand and choked back another laugh. 'I can't believe you said that.'

'Caitlin,' he had said, his voice roughening as he said her name, 'I'm quite serious. I've wanted you for years. If you hadn't been such a damned little fool about Luke, you'd have known how I felt.'

'Why would you say such a thing to me?' she had said nervously, watching his face. 'You've got all the women you could want; you never made that a secret.'

'None of those women mean a thing to me,' he had said, moving towards her. 'You can eat and still be hungry, drink and still be thirsty, Caitlin. Do you understand? You're the only woman I ever really wanted.'

'Don't touch me,' she had said sharply.

'You never once looked at me the way you looked at my brother, did you? I was just part of the scenery. You were like all the rest, fawning over him, ignoring me.'

'I loved Luke ...'

'You loved Luke,' he had repeated mockingly. 'The truth is that you liked the taste of power, once you inherited your puny five percent and got a piece of it. Well, I'm offering you a chance to have it all, Caitlin. You can keep Thomas Pharmaceuticals just the way it is and share in the power if you become my wife.'

Caitlin had swallowed the bitterness welling in her throat. 'You're sick,' she had whispered.

'Just think about it, Caitlin,' he had said, pausing a breath away from her. 'Marry me, and I'll agree to forget about selling out to Clarke. I'll keep the damned research lab—I'll even set up that fellowship in Luke's name.'

'This is insane,' she had murmured. 'Do you really think I could ever want you, Justin?'

'It's what I want that matters now, my dear.'

'I'd never agree to such a marriage. Never, Justin.'

He had smiled and sat down on the edge of a table piled high with account ledgers. 'Do you see these, Caitlin?' he had asked, gesturing to the stack of books. 'They tell the story of Thomas Pharmaceuticals, past and present. It's the future you hold in your hands, my dear. You're good at working out balance sheets, aren't you? Well, try this equation. On the one side, a continuation of Thomas, with the added benefit of a Luke Thomas Graduate Research Fellowship—and on the other side, a buy-out by Clarke Labs. Now, which do you think Luke would have preferred?'

'Justin,' she had pleaded desperately, 'don't do this. If you sell out, everything Luke worked for, died for, will vanish. Please . . .'

'I offered you a rather generous proposition a few minutes ago, Caitlin. Perhaps you'd care to reconsider it.'

'You're vile,' she had whispered. 'Luke's memory is all I have left.'

'Since that's what you believe to be true, my dear, we're in complete agreement. If all you have left for comfort is my brother's martyred memory you have to consider my offer, don't you?'

Caitlin had looked at him warily from under the dark sweep of her lashes. 'This must be some sort of macabre joke. You're not serious, Justin.'

'I'm quite serious,' he had said pleasantly.

She had known, suddenly, that every word he had uttered was the truth. 'Justin,' she had said carefully, searching without success for the words to tell him what she thought of him, 'you . . . you are a . . . a . . .'

'I'm sure the proper phrase will come to you in due time, Caitlin. Meanwhile, I have a meeting in an hour with a gentleman from Clarke. He wants to discuss our current non-prescription inventory, and he wants to know more about that new line of antibiotics we brought into production. You know the ones, Luke took some of them to Central America with him. He planned to distribute them in some god-forsaken Asian country, too, but I think I'll tell this gentleman that it doesn't really pay to do that; they'll do better in a limited, more lucrative market.' He smiled lazily at her. 'Well, no matter. Clarke will make those decisions soon enough. Unless of course, you choose to make a decision of your own.' Slowly, he had walked to the door and hesitated. 'Just think of the power you hold in those delicate hands, Caitlin. Do we, you and I, run this company, or do I sell it to the highest bidder?'

'Damn you, Justin.'

'Probably,' he had said agreeably, laughing at her. 'I don't want you to feel rushed, Caitlin. Why don't you give me your answer in a day or so?'

'I can give it to you right now,' she had said fiercely. 'I'll never marry you, Justin. Never.'

But, within twenty-four hours, calls had begun to reach her from business associates who offered their condolences and then hesitantly asked if the rumours about the sale of Thomas were true. In less than a day, everything Luke had worked for was fragmenting, vanishing in Justin's greed and jealousy. She had pleaded with him until she was hoarse, argued until there were no arguments left to offer, to no end.

The day on which she was to begin readying the firm's books for the Clarke accountants had dawned uncharacteristically grey and cool. The heavy skies and chill wind had seemed a mirror of her own despair. Caitlin had reached her office early, and in the empty silence, she had sat motionless at her desk, staring with vacant eyes at the papers awaiting her. Her glance had fallen upon a preliminary report from the experimental lab: they'd had limited success with the new vaccine Luke had been so excited about, but what did it matter? Soon, such work would be cast aside. And there, lying next to it, had been a scrawled, worried note from someone in the order department telling her Justin had denied a request for shipment of drugs to a small hospital in India. Caitlin had closed her eyes and covered them with her hands. Even the brief, simple funeral service they'd held over the urn of ashes that had been shipped home had not seemed as final as seeing the total dissolution of Luke's dreams.

Suddenly, she had raised her head and pushed aside the papers that littered her desk. Afraid her courage would fail her, she had hurried across the hall until she stood before the door to Justin's office. Taking a final, deep breath, she had squared her shoulders and pushed the door open. Justin had turned in surprise as she entered.

'I won't tolerate any more discussion, Caitlin,' he had said immediately. 'You're to get started on those figures this morning.'

'You win,' she had said without explanation. 'I'll marry you.'

A look of triumph had passed across his face. 'An astute decision, Caitlin,' he had said finally.

'I want a guaranteed payment, Justin. I won't go through with this unless I'm convinced that the company will remain intact and there will be a fellowship set up in Luke's name.'

He had smiled mockingly. 'You have my word of honour.'

Her laughter had been brief and shrill. 'Your word of honour? You'll have to do better than that, Justin. I want a pre-nuptial agreement, setting out our terms. And you're going to assign the voting rights to Luke's stock to me before we marry.'

'That's ridiculous, Caitlin.'

'That's the way it will be, Justin,' she had said firmly, trying to still the pounding of her heart as she faced him. 'If I'm to be the price of Luke's dream, then it will have to be worth more than your honour. You said you wanted me; well, let's see how much you really meant it.'

His eyes had met hers unflinchingly. After a long silence, he had grinned and pulled her to him.

'Agreed,' he had said hoarsely. 'There's a toughness in you, Caitlin, a fire that needs taming, and I'm the man to do do it.' Abruptly, his hot mouth had descended on hers and she had forced herself to withstand the pressure of his lips.

'I hate you, Justin,' she had whispered when he released her. 'Nothing will ever change that.'

'I'll change it, my dear,' he had assured her, running his fingers along her jaw as she stood unmoving. 'I know you better than you suspect, Caitlin. Someday, you'll want me just as I want you. And when that day comes, when you've put this rather charming if somewhat misplaced dedication to Luke behind us, we'll discuss the future of Thomas Pharmaceuticals again.'

'We'll never discuss it,' she had said sharply. 'Not once we sign our agreement. You'll have what you want, and I'll do what you forced me to do. And we'll both live with the bargain we made.'

'From this day forward,' he had muttered, and she had shuddered as she thought of how obscene those old-fashioned words from the marriage ceremony had become once he had uttered them.

The piercing rasp of a fog-horn interrupted Caitlin's thoughts. She brushed the tears from her eyes and stared blindly at the Seine glistening in the faint moonlight. The pre-nuptial agreement had been drawn up and signed, Justin had named her the heir to his own stock, and Thomas Pharmaceuticals had continued to function as it always had. The Luke Thomas Fellowship had already funded two promising young scientists. Caitlin had not regretted the choice she'd made—until this evening.

'Oh, Luke,' she whispered sadly into the bleak silence of the Paris night, 'how could you have believed Justin? How could you have stopped loving me?'

But the silent, dark night offered no answers. In the last, lingering hour before the first touch of a grey dawn lit the mute sky, she slowly retraced her steps to the hotel.

CHAPTER FOUR

AT nine o'clock that morning, Caitlin knocked on the door of Emily Thomas's suite.

'Come in, Caitlin, for heaven's sake,' the old woman said peevishly, pulling the door open and stepping aside. 'We'd almost given up hope of seeing you.'

'Good morning, Aunt Emily,' Caitlin said pleasantly, bending to kiss the wrinkled cheek offered to her and nodding at Emily's son, Warren, who was lounging casually in an overstuffed chair. 'I'm not late, am I? We did agree to meet at nine.'

'I want to begin promptly, Caitlin,' Emily Thomas sniffed. 'Warren, sit up straight and get your feet on the floor. This is a business meeting, in case you'd forgotten. Sit down, Caitlin, sit down,' she said, impatiently waving at a chair drawn up before the coffee table. 'Have you brought all those figures I asked to see?'

Caitlin sighed and deposited a stack of printouts on the table. 'Yes, all of them. I still would prefer to meet in the conference room, Aunt Emily. We'd have more space and it would be much easier to go through these papers.'

Emily sipped at her coffee and shrugged her shoulders. 'I don't need to go through them. Warren has done all that already. I just want to be able to point out some things to you. Evian is quite a nice little company, isn't it?'

'They really aren't doing as well as they'd like us to think,' Caitlin said quickly. 'But before we get to that, something's happened that you should know about.'

Warren Thomas stretched his arms over his head and smiled. 'Do try those croissants with the wild-strawberry jam, Caitlin. They're divine.' He leaned forward and stirred his coffee. 'If it's about Cousin Luke, we already know, don't we, Mother? Wonderful news for all of us, isn't it?'

Caitlin looked up and her eyes searched Warren's face. The expression on it didn't quite match the sound of his words.

'When did you find out, Warren?'

'Last night, just after dinner, wasn't it, Mother?' Warren smiled again and reached for the Spode creamer. 'Who would have dreamed such a thing, hmm? You must be delighted, Caitlin.'

'Of course,' she said stiffly, looking away from him. 'It must have been quite a shock for you, Emily.'

The old lady nodded. 'Indeed it was. But, of course, it was wonderful to see him again. I asked him to join us this morning—I trust you have no objections. After all, until the legalities are all cleared up, he has no voting privileges, but he certainly has an interest in these proceedings.' She glanced shrewdly at Caitlin over the tops of the half-frame reading glasses perched on her nose. 'He'll be wanting his shares back, of course,' she said flatly.

'He's entitled to them, Caitlin,' Warren said primly, when she made no response. 'Surely you see that.'

Caitlin bit her lip and leafed through a small notebook in her lap. 'We discussed that possibility, Warren. But that isn't what we're here to talk about just now, is it? About this merger...'

'Luke thinks it's an excellent idea,' Emily interrupted. 'He agrees with us.'

'Then he doesn't know all the facts. This company only wants to use us to get a foot in the American market. They've inflated their profits to look good, far better than they really are. And some of their policies are the exact opposite of ours.'

'Nonsense,' Emily snapped. 'You just don't want to lose your hold on the company, Caitlin. You're afraid that's precisely what will happen when we merge.'

'If we merge,' Caitlin countered. 'Nothing's been decided yet.'

'I tell you Luke agrees with us, Caitlin. We want the deal to go through, and we're sure we can persuade the others. If we can't—and if you continue to oppose us—we'll wait until Luke regains rightful control of his shares and we'll not only outvote you, we'll replace you.'

Caitlin stood so quickly that her notebook tumbled from her lap. 'Don't count on it,' she said quietly. 'If that's what Luke promised you, you'd better not hold your breath. I'm sorry to upset everybody's plans, but Luke will need an attorney to get that stock from me, and by the time this gets to court, Evian will have lost all interest in Thomas Pharmaceuticals.'

'Well, well, Caitlin,' a sarcastic voice drawled. 'I can see why Emily warned me about you. You really are full of fight, aren't you?'

She spun around and saw Luke staring at her from just inside the doorway. 'I didn't hear you come in.'

He smiled coolly. 'How could you? You were too busy making that terrific speech.'

'Is she right, Luke?' Emily asked petulantly. 'Will it take a long time to get your stock back?'

He shrugged and continued staring at Caitlin. 'Probably long enough for Evian to have faded into the woodwork by then. That is, unless we can persuade Caitlin to give up gracefully.'

She bent and retrieved her notebook, giving herself time to recover her composure. 'It's not a question of giving up, Emily,' she said, ignoring Luke completely. 'I'm not worried about losing anything.'

The brittle sound of Luke's laughter cut through the quiet room. 'No? That's not quite accurate, is it? I mean, we all know how much trouble you went to so you could get control of this company in the first place.'

'Luke...'

'So it seems reasonable to assume you won't give up easily now,' he continued, his hazel eyes seeming to burn through her. 'From what Emily and Warren told me, you're opposed to this deal strictly because it will probably topple you from your throne. That's not a pretty prospect for you to contemplate, is it, Cat?'

She snatched up the computer printouts and stalked rapidly across the room. 'Why don't you look these over before you start making accusations?' she demanded angrily. 'Or are you afraid to find out that you're wrong?' Taking a deep, calming breath, she fought to control her voice. 'I don't know what Emily told you, Luke, but I do know you haven't seen these figures. I can't get them to listen to reason, but maybe you can.' Suddenly, she became aware of how close she was to him, and the amused, almost contemptuous look on his face, and she shuddered involuntarily. 'I know what you think of me,' she said, so quietly that only he could hear her. 'But I beg you to go over these papers before you make up your mind.'

'All right, Cat,' he said, taking them from her. 'Don't worry Emily,' he added as his aunt began to sputter with displeasure. 'It won't take very long, and I think we owe Caitlin that much, considering all she's done for the company.'

The mocking tone in his voice made her cheeks flush, but she managed a polite smile.

'Thank you,' she said. 'Let me know if you want to see any other documents.'

Luke grinned and raised his eyebrows. 'How

accommodating you are this morning, sister-in-law. As a matter of fact, I'd like to see the firm's accounts for this year and last, and a list of products in production, plus whatever you have on their new drug research.' He paused and his glance swept her face. 'I'm sure you could quote it all to me, chapter and verse, but I'd rather see it for myself.' Again, the grin twisted his mouth. 'Not that I don't trust you, Cat...'

She ignored the faint sound of Warren's laughter and opened the door. 'I'll have my secretary bring everything to you in the conference room in half an hour,' she said calmly.

'Your suite will be just fine,' he said, closing the door behind them. 'I don't want to inconvenience you, my dear sister-in-law, and I don't want you to go to all the trouble of sifting through those records. You might just leave something behind—inadvertently, of course.'

Caitlin stopped short and swung around to confront him. 'First of all,' she said rapidly. 'You can just stop calling me that.'

'Sister-in-law?' he asked innocently. 'But that's what you are, Cat.'

'Just stop it, Luke. And I'd appreciate an end to all these ... these veiled hints that I'm trying to hide the facts. By all means, come to my suite with me. You can go over anything you like; I won't lay a hand on a single sheet of paper.'

Three hours later, she sat quietly curled on a corner of the couch in her sitting room, watching Luke as he went through the documents. Except for a few brief questions, he'd said nothing to her from the time they'd entered her suite. Caitlin sipped at a cup of coffee and thought of how often they'd sat like this before, one of them intent on some new project while the other waited eagerly to discuss it. And yet, of course, this was quite different.

Last night, in the painful anger of their meeting, she had sworn to hold on to the stock for which she'd paid so dearly. And in the hours after dawn, alone again in her rooms, she'd made peace with herself. The four years of her life that she'd given to the nurturing of a memory would become meaningless if she let him give away his company out of anger at her. And it was his company, she reminded herself, glancing over at him again. She had never thought of herself as anything but its custodian.

Luke pushed his chair back from the table and tossed his pencil aside. Wearily, he flexed his shoulders and then reached into his pocket for a cigarette.

'I'll take that cup of coffee now,' he said, turning to face her. 'Just a little cream, no . . .'

'No sugar,' Caitlin said automatically, handing him a cup. 'I remember.'

He glanced up at her and she flushed and turned away, busying herself with refilling her own cup from the elaborate Georgian coffee service.

'Well?' she asked. 'Does the merger with Evian still look as great as Emily and Warren think?'

He sighed and pushed his dark brown hair off his forehead with an all-too-familiar gesture. 'No, not quite,' he admitted. 'You were right, Cat. There are more questions than there are answers. What did your accountant say when he finished with this stuff?'

Relief flooded through her. She had not been sure, until this moment, that his feelings towards her wouldn't warp his assessment of Evian. She sat down opposite him and sipped at her coffee.

'He agreed that Evian isn't sitting on top of the world. Their profit figures are inflated, and it's also possible they've overextended themselves considerably. He couldn't comment on their research and production policies, that's really a management issue. But he pointed out there were things we could gain from the merger—a European branch, a larger market. He suggested I could use what we know to get a better deal from Evian.'

Luke blew a series of tiny smoke rings towards the ceiling, tilting his head back to watch them as they vanished against the cream-coloured paint.

'And? What did you decide?'

'I don't want any part of Evian, Luke.' Caitlin tossed her hair back from her face and bent over the papers sprawled before them, pointing to a large spread sheet. 'Our operating profit margin should continue to rise next year, and you can see for yourself the upswing in our price/earnings ratio. A merger with Evian will drop all these projections, if I'm right about their cash flow and the mistakes they've made in capital expenditures.'

Luke glanced up at her and an enigmatic smile crossed his face. 'You're pretty comfortable with all of this, aren't you, Cat? The formulas, the ratios, the projections are tucked away into that pretty head of yours like stuff stored inside a computer.'

'Why should that surprise you?' she said quickly. 'The company is important to me. That's why I'm so opposed to the merger.'

He leaned back and looked at her thoughtfully, fingers playing a soft tattoo on the table top.

'Still,' he said finally, his words almost a whisper, 'you could go ahead with it. There are reasons you might want to.'

'What reasons? Evian isn't worth anywhere near what it claims, I'm certain. In fact, I don't think their prospects are any too good.' She sighed tiredly and put down her coffee cup. 'I'd have turned them down flat, but Emily insisted on this meeting, and she persuaded some of the others to go along.'

She waited for him to answer. After several seconds, she looked up and her eyes met his. For the first time since he'd returned, there was no hostility in his glance.

'Your accountant is right, you know, Cat. You could probably use what you suspect to gain some leverage, maybe even enough to assure yourself of the top spot in the set-up after the merger is completed.'

Caitlin slammed her hand down on the table. 'That's not what I'm interested in doing,' she said, her voice shrill with tired exasperation. 'How many times do I have to explain?'

Luke's eyes raked over her face, and then he shrugged and ground out his cigarette. 'I'm trying to understand, Cat. For a woman who doesn't let anything slip through her fingers, you seem strangely willing to give up something that could benefit you. This deal, even with its pitfalls, could mean lots of money, prestige, all the things you're interested in.'

'How do you know what interests me?' she demanded angrily, getting to her feet and staring down at him. 'You come back after almost four years, full of self-righteous anger, certain you have all the answers to everything ... well. Luke Thomas, you *don't* know it all. Especially when it comes to my interests.' She was horrified to feel tears in her eyes, and she turned away quickly before he could see their telltale glisten. 'The important thing is to tell Emily that you agree with me,' she said, dabbing at her eyes before turning to face him again. 'And your cousins when they get here. They'll listen to you.'

Luke stretched lazily and stood up. 'I haven't said I agree with you, Cat,' he said carefully. 'I have to know more about Evian before that. And there are other questions ...'

'What other questions?'

'Ones you won't like. For instance, why are you so damned eager to get me on your side, Cat? Last night, you almost threw me out of your suite, but today . . .'

'Today, all that counts is saving the character of Thomas Pharmaceuticals.'

He smiled grimly and moved towards her. 'Such lofty sentiments,' he murmured. 'And it all sounds so selfless, coming from that beautiful face.'

'Luke . . .'

'You'll forgive me if I don't quite buy it, won't you, Cat? Maybe I don't know all the answers, but I sure as hell know that you're covering up something with all this talk of saving the company. I can't help but wonder exactly what it is you stand to gain if I throw my support in with you.' He reached out and took her roughly by the shoulders. 'What is it you haven't told me, Cat?'

Caitlin shook her head and felt the tears begin to trace a pathway down her cheeks. 'Nothing,' she said desperately, trying unsuccessfully to pull free of his hands. 'Look, I'll make a deal with you, Luke. Back me on this, and as soon as the vote is taken, after I've won, I'll turn the stock over to you.'

His eyes narrowed until she could see only their gold and green specks. 'I told you not to take me for a fool,' he warned.

'I'm not,' she insisted. 'I just want us out of this merger. Then I'll step aside, Luke. I promise.'

'All you're doing is convincing me that you have another card up your sleeve,' he growled, his fingers biting into her skin.

'I haven't, I swear,' she said, but his disbelief was etched in the hard lines around his mouth. 'All right,' she lied, her mind a whirl of desperate plans and half-formed ideas. 'I . . . I have a better offer, Luke. Clarke Labs offered me a position. More money, more prestige . . . it won't look good to them if I can't control my own board on an issue like this merger. I need your help to nail down that offer.' The lie was bitter on her tongue, but she prayed he would believe it.

'That sounds more like it,' he muttered. 'Is there a man involved, too? After all, that's one of your specialities, isn't it? You wanted Thomas so badly that you used me, and then my brother, to get it.'

With a wrench, she pulled free of his unwelcome grasp. 'That's not the way it was,' she said wearily. 'I loved you, Luke.'

'Sure you did,' he said thickly. 'So much that you married Justin before I was cold in my grave. Poor Justin—what you must have done to him to make him propose so quickly. Did you threaten to run off and leave? Or did you give him just enough of those teasing kisses and touches to drive him crazy?'

Her hand swung up and slapped his face. The sound hung between them like the sharp retort of a bullet. Luke raised his hand and Caitlin drew in her breath, waiting for him to retaliate, but instead his hand closed around the back of her neck, pulling her closer to him.

'That found the mark, didn't it, Cat? Innocent little Caitlin, making the most of her lovely face, her beautiful body, and then striking fast, making sure my brother wouldn't change his mind.'

'That's a lie,' she whispered. 'I'd never do anything like that.'

'I know just what you'd do, Cat,' he said softly, his murmured words a warm breath on her cheek. 'God knows you did it to me. And I know you tried the same stuff on him. He told me how you flirted with him.'

'Never!' she said sharply. 'I was in love with you . . .'

'You were in love with power, Cat. I even punched Justin once, did you know that? I couldn't face the simple, ugly truth even when he tried to show it to me. I didn't want to hear that your soft mouth, your kisses, offered nothing but lies.' Without warning, his mouth descended on hers, but it was a kiss empty of warmth or love, and she struggled in his embrace.

'Let go of me, Luke,' she whispered desperately. 'Don't do this.'

'Don't do what?' he demanded harshly. 'You want something from me, don't you? Well then, why not pay for it in your usual coin.'

Caitlin's body went limp in his hard, cold embrace. 'I can't believe I ever loved you,' she murmured, raising her eyes to his. 'I never thought I'd feel the way I do this minute.'

His lips pulled back from his teeth in a wolfish grin. 'Are you telling me it's no deal, Cat?'

'I offered you a bargain,' she said, fighting against the tears of anger and sorrow welling in her eyes. 'I'll turn my ... your stock over to you in exchange for your backing.'

'It's not enough,' he said quickly. 'I want Justin's stock, too. I think that's only fair, don't you?'

She drew a ragged breath and nodded. 'I don't want any of it.'

His hands dropped from her shoulders. 'I suppose I'll have to be satisfied with that, won't I? But I don't quite trust you, sweet Caitlin. Matter of fact, I can't think of any reason why I should.'

'You have no choice,' she said quickly. 'Part of the merger deal involves some of the Evian stock, you know. A lot of it will go to me, and there's nothing you can do about it. And then, of course,' she added swiftly, praying he'd believe her, 'I'll fight you. I'm at least entitled to Justin's stock. Any court will agree to that, and I suspect my lawyers will put up a tough fight against you. Even if you get your own holdings back, it'll be a long time before it happens.'

He looked at her, a cigarette dangling from his lips, his eyes narrowed against the smoke. 'I've got to hand it to you, Cat. You really know how to drive a bargain.'

'Then you'll do it?'

'Only because it's the fastest way I know of to wipe you out of my life forever,' he growled.

'A sweet sense of relief flooded through her. 'Well, then,' she said slowly, 'I guess I'll see you next week.'

'No such luck, Cat. I'll see you tomorrow, bright and early. I want to go over and visit the Evian lab.'

'There's no reason for that.'

He grinned mirthlessly and straightened his tie. 'I at least want a look at the place before I commit myself to this. Don't look so worried, Cat. Unless it turns out to be some kind of technological miracle, I'll keep our bargain.'

Caitlin sank down onto a chair and leaned her head back. 'Go by yourself, then,' she said wearily. 'I don't think either of us wants to be in the company of the other.'

'Absolutely right, Mrs Thomas. But I want the top level, executive-only tour, the kind you can get. So just be ready first thing in the morning, will you? That way, we won't be stuck with each other for the entire day.'

She nodded resolutely, her face a worn, grim mask until the door slammed shut behind him. Then, like a marionette cut free of its strings, she slumped over and bowed her head.

Had there ever really been love between them, she wondered? Often enough, in the past, he'd asked her if she was sure she'd given herself a chance to know that what had begun between them when she was still in college wasn't just a schoolgirl's crush. Always, she'd assured him that she loved him. Now she wondered if perhaps she'd never known the real man. Still, she thought, wiping tears of frustration from her face, the company was his. If her unholy alliance with Justin was to have any meaning Thomas Pharmaceuticals must remain intact until its return to its rightful owner.

'Only a few more days,' she whispered aloud. 'I can live through just a few more days after these last four years. And then, Luke Thomas, I'll never have to see you again.'

The thought, as her mind formed it, had great conviction and finality. But somehow, as the words drifted through the empty room, they seemed more a cry of pain than a determined pledge.

CHAPTER FIVE

EVIAN ET FRERES was located in a gleaming new building on the outskirts of the city. The general manager greeted Caitlin and Luke warmly, although he seemed surprised to learn that they wanted to tour the laboratory facilities. He suggested they might prefer to meet with the laboratory director in his office over coffee and pastries, but Caitlin was politely insistent. Finally, he scurried ahead of them, leading them down long, antiseptically white corridors and in and out of rooms lined with gleaming equipment. He answered their questions carefully, deferring to the biologists and chemists in the labs when the answers required more technical skill, helping pleasantly with the difficult translations of data from English to French and back again to English.

'Lot's of equipment, but not enough personnel,' Luke muttered to Caitlin at one point, when they were out of the manager's hearing.

'Yes, I think so, too. It points up what I suspected—they must have overextended themselves when they built this place last year.'

Eventually, when they'd completed their circuit of the building, Caitlin thanked the manager for his courtesy and she and Luke headed back into the street.

'Emily is going to be looking for me,' Luke said, hailing a passing taxi. 'And I really don't want to see her just yet. Look, Cat, we've managed to avoid fighting with each other for the last three hours. How about stretching our luck and stopping for lunch somewhere? I'd like to go over what we've just seen before I have to answer any questions from Emily or Warren.'

She hesitated only a second and then she nodded. 'Yes, I suppose that would be a good idea. Emily will probably pounce on you as soon as she knows we're back.'

He leaned forward to give an address to the driver, and the taxi fought its way into the swift-running river of Parisian traffic. Caitlin sat stiffly on the far side of the small car, grateful for the shrill horn blasts and roaring engines that made conversation all but impossible. She glanced over at Luke. He seemed absorbed in thought and completely unaware of her presence. Again, she noticed the scar along his cheek, and a wave of compassion for him and the ordeal he'd survived washed over her. His face was relaxed, his mouth firm yet as gentle-looking as she'd always remembered it, the hard lines bracketing it smoothed and almost indiscernible. She thought of all the times she'd felt the touch of that mouth on hers and a rush of colour suffused her face. Almost angrily, she turned her head away, staring blindly out of the window as the taxi wove its way through the crowded streets, reminding herself with unforgiving clarity that those memories were part of the distant past.

Caitlin closed her eyes and leaned her head back against the worn seat. Until the other night she'd never doubted his love for her. And yet, now that she thought about it, why hadn't he asked her to set a date for their wedding? And why had he drawn back each time they came close to losing themselves in each other's arms? It had always seemed such a protective, gentle gesture; he'd whisper that he was willing to wait until she was really his.

'I've had nine years more of living than you, Cat,' he'd said the first time they talked of marriage. 'I want you to be sure this is what you want.'

Had his concern for her only masked his own indecision? Was he, even then, falling victim to Justin's lies and accusations? No, she thought quickly, that wasn't possible. Luke had loved her; she had to believe that. Cautiously, she opened her eyes and risked another look at him. He looked tired, she thought suddenly, and older than he should. For a second, her questions and confusion vanished, driven from her by an almost overwhelming need to reach out and touch him, cradle him in her arms and ease those lines from his face. And yet . . . and yet . . . She could forgive him the other woman he'd known, even forgive him his doubts about her, but to what end? His love for her had proved to be as fragile and as transitory as a bubble on a pond: gleaming and whole in the sunlight, but collapsed and forgotten in the first toss of the wind.

She sat up a bit straighter and moved farther into the corner of the seat.

'How did you hear about the merger?' she asked, to bridge the silence.

He turned towards her, his eyes glazed with some distant vision.

'What? Oh, I told you I phoned my lawyer. I told the Consul that I had to get to Paris just as soon as he could fix me up with a passport. He argued a bit; he wanted me to take it easy for a while. Anyway, as soon as my lawyer wired me some money, I got on the first plane out.'

'Jean—my secretary—picked up a couple of American newspapers the other day. I'd have thought your escape would have been front-page news.'

A faint, impersonal smile touched his face. 'Yeah, I guess it would have, but I talked the Consul into agreeing to hold off on notifying the press. I told him I wanted the pleasure of breaking the news to the folks back home all by myself.'

She flushed at the sarcastic ring to the innocent words. 'Your escape ... you said that you slipped away one night. It must have taken you days to reach the city.'

He stretched his long legs out before him and shrugged. 'I was pretty well prepared for it,' he said easily. 'It was rough, but I was determined to make it. I had a canteen, some cold tortillas, some dried meat, just enough to stay alive. Maria had stashed some supplies for me just outside the village.'

'She must have ... cared for you a great deal,' Caitlin finally answered.

'Yeah, she was terrific,' he said gruffly. 'Anyway, I made it. Just in time to help you save the company from making a disastrous move.'

A sharp wave of relief washed over her. 'You agree with me about Evian?'

He nodded his head and smiled. 'Yes, Evian is definitely bad news.'

'Thank you,' she said simply. 'I'm so glad to hear that.'

'I guess you are, Cat. You must want that job in Los Angeles pretty badly.'

'The job in ...' She looked at him blankly and then she blushed and smiled stiffly. 'Of course I do,' she said quickly.

'Kind of funny it should be Clarke that wants you, isn't it? Just a few years ago, you were trying to persuade me to sell out to them, remember?'

'Luke, I just wanted you to be free of Justin.'

He smiled and lit a cigarette. 'Yes, so you said. Oh, I believed you, Cat,' he added when she began to protest. 'Even though Justin insisted you really wanted the money, I believed you. Although I'd have thought Clarke would have tried to buy out Thomas's again, once they knew I was out of the picture.'

'Well, they didn't,' she said stiffly. 'But they did offer me a position I want. That's why I need your help now.'

He chuckled and shifted in his seat until he faced her. 'It's hard to picture you needing anybody's help. Don't get your back up, Cat. That was a compliment. I spent a lot of time going through those reports you gave me. You've done a fine job managing the company.'

She looked at him in surprise, searching his face for some concealed double meaning, but the look he gave her was one of honest admiration.

'Thank you,' she said cautiously.

'I mean it, Cat. You streamlined some lab operations, I noticed. And you picked up some solid new accounts. There's no harm in admitting you handled things well. Gaining control of a corporation and being able to deal with it aren't necessarily the same thing.'

'I didn't plan on gaining control,' she said sharply. 'How many times must I tell you that?'

'I'm not trying to pick a fight with you,' he said, tossing his cigarette butt out of the window. 'All I'm trying to do is thank you for having done a good job.'

'I don't want your gratitude,' she said stiffly. 'I just did what had to be done.'

'Well, whatever you did, it worked, and I'd be a fool to deny it. At least, I have something left to come home to.'

Because of me, she thought fiercely, biting back the words. Because I loved you more than you can imagine. Because, even now, after all you've said, knowing what you believe me capable of, I can't stop remembering what we once had. Because I'm a fool, she thought with finality, angered by her own weakness. She settled back in the seat, grimly determined to get through lunch as quickly as possible.

The streets grew more congested as they neared the centre of the city, and the cab moved forward in ragged surges of speed as the driver took full advantage of each break in the traffic. Muttering an oath under his breath, in the time-honoured tradition of cabbies on both sides of the Atlantic, he swerved sharply to avoid a pedestrain, just as a fast-moving motorcycle cut ahead of them. The brakes squealed as the cab stopped just short of disaster, and Caitlin was flung unceremoniously across the seat and against Luke.

'I'm sorry,' she stammered, scuttling back to her side of the cab. 'I . . .'

Her embarrassed explanation caught in her throat as she looked at Luke's face. He was intent on something that had caught his eye on the sidewalk, and there was such a naked look of pain in the twist of his mouth and the narrowing of his eyes that she almost reached out to him.

'Luke,' she whispered, 'what is it?'

He shook his head abruptly, not answering her, and her gaze followed his out of the window. She drew in her breath a she saw what he was staring at.

There was a cinema a short distance from them; huge posters announced the première showing of a new American film. Luke's eye were riveted on a placard mounted near the entrance to the theatre. It showed a young couple walking hand in hand along a deserted beach, their footsteps leading down from what could only be a cliff at Big Sur on the California coast. The sun-warmed girl in the picture leaned against the man's side in the same way she had so often leaned against Luke while they walked along the clean, white sand, filled with the sheer pleasure of being one with the sea, the sky, and each other.

The traffic moved forward again and the cab leaped ahead with a noisy grinding of its gears. Caitlin sat silently, her thoughts turned inwards, memories swirling around her like the eddies of the ocean sweeping upon the hot, white sand.

Beside her, Luke stirred and cleared his throat. 'Caitlin . . .' he said hoarsely, and she turned towards him blindly.

'*Le Procope, monsieur,*' the driver announced, pulling the cab to the curb. '*Nous sommes arrivé au restaurant,*' he added, when neither of them responded.

Caitlin's words were a faint whisper. 'He says . . .'

'Yes, I know. We're here.' Luke swung open the door and stepped out on to the sidewalk.

Caitlin hurried past him, not waiting while he paid the driver, barely noticing the handsome old building facing her. Its broad windows, filled with posters, made the façade come alive with colour, but the effect was lost on her. She was blind to everything but the image of Luke's face as it had been only moments before. It was as if a mask had been stripped from his features, revealing some hidden core of him. If only the moment had lasted longer, she thought wildly, as she walked with him into a small, elegant dining room. It was as though she had been stopped from opening the tiny, last box hidden within a nest of boxes.

They were seated at a table next to a window overlooking the street. Caitlin accepted the menu from the waitress and studied it unseeingly. Cautiously, she raised her eyes and risked a glance across the table at Luke, only to find him staring at her.

'What are you thinking?' he asked in a subdued tone.

Her pulse seemed to quicken, and she fought back the sudden desire to tell him that she loved him, that what she had seen on his face in the cab had given her a second of crazy, desperate hope that he still loved her, too.

'I was thinking . . .' She paused, waiting until she trusted herself to go on. 'I was thinking how happy I am that you're back, that you're alive and well.'

'Are you?' he asked, leaning across the pale pink tablecloth and searching her eyes with his. 'Even after the other night . . .'

'Yes,' she murmured, the colour rising swiftly to her cheeks. 'When I opened the door and saw you standing there, it seemed like a miracle. Only a little while before, I'd been working with Jean, going over some details about Evian, and she started talking about Paris . . .' Caitlin swallowed the lump that had risen in her throat and looked down at the table. 'I started thinking about you,' she whispered, 'about you and all the times we talked about coming to Paris together.'

She forced herself to look at him again. Something seemed to light the hidden depths in his eyes, and she held her breath, wondering what he might say.

'Yes, I understand,' he said finally. 'Remembering is painful sometimes. There are some things we try to deny, but it's impossible. Just a few minutes ago, in that cab . . .'

'I saw the poster, too,' she said softly.

He nodded his head and stared at her. 'We had some great times together, didn't we, Cat? he murmured. 'We were like that couple in the picture, wealking along the beach, alone in our own world.'

Tears blurred her eyes and she fought for self-control before she dared answer.

'I was afraid you'd forgotten how it was between us, Luke,' she whispered.

'No,' he said carefully, picking up the wine list from

the table, 'I haven't forgotten. I wish I could, Cat. It only confuses things to remember.'

She leaned forward across the table. 'It doesn't have to,' she said quickly.'

'But it does,' he said evenly, not looking up from the wine list. He motioned to the nearby waitress and ordered an estate-bottled Vouvray in faltering French. 'It does,' he repeated after she had moved away from the table. 'I want my life to move forward again, Cat,' he said, his voice thick and hesitant. 'And the only way that can happen is to close the book on the past.'

Caitlin nodded, trying to collect her thoughts, afraid to puncture the fragile bond forming between them.

'I guess that makes sense,' she said at last. 'But no one can separate the past from the present, or the present from the future. Each leads to the other. What I'm trying to say is that you can't set the past aside until you understand it.'

He lit a cigarette and drew on it before he spoke. 'Look, Cat, we don't have to talk in riddles. We both know you're talking about you and Justin.'

'Luke . . .'

'And the way it used to be for us. Believe me, I understand everything I have to understand.'

'But you don't,' she said quickly.

His eyes raked over her face and a muscle tensed in his jaw. 'Sure I do,' he said finally. 'You made it clear the other night, remember? You said you were glad it was Justin you married, because he was twice the man I ever was.'

Caitlin flinched at the raw sound of her own desperate, angry words as he repeated them to her.

'That was a lie,' she whispered unhappily, her eyes pleading with his for understanding. 'You said such terrible things to me that night . . . I was so hurt that I wanted to hurt you, too.'

A half-smile curved at the corners of his mouth. 'Yeah, well you succeeded. There I was, giving it my best shot, and you went straight for my jugular.'

'Well, what did you expect?' she asked quickly, a defensive tone toughening her voice. 'You pushed me, until . . .'

'I know,' he said quickly. 'It got a little out of hand, I guess. But you came at me like a wildcat. It was an impressive performance.'

In spite of herself, she returned his smile. 'Was that a compliment? If it was, it's the second one you've given me in the past hour.'

'Prepare yourself for a third,' he murmured, as their waitress approached the table carrying a wine bucket. 'Help me make some sense out of this menu, will you? Once I've ordered *vin*, *café*, and *croissants*, I've gone about as far as I can on my own.'

Caitlin nodded and translated the luncheon suggestions the waitress offered in rapid French, trying not to admit to herself how wonderful it was to be with him. It was difficult to compare this man with the one who had confronted her in her suite the other night. It almost seemed as if the old Luke she remembered had surfaced for a flickering second after they'd seen that cinema poster. If only . . . She looked up in confusion, aware that he was speaking to her.

'I'm sorry?' she said quickly.

'I said I was amazed the waitress brought the Vouvray I ordered, Cat. That's the trouble with not speaking a language well. You can never be certain that what you get is what you asked for.'

The deeper truth in his words stung her. How many times had she dreamed of having him back, alive and well? But never like this, never without his loving her. He filled their glasses with the pale wine and she raised hers with a slightly unsteady hand.

'What shall we drink to?' she asked quietly.

He smiled slightly and touched his glass to hers. 'To our combined efforts against Evian and Emily, I suppose.'

It was foolish to have expected anything more, she thought, forcing herself to return his smile.

'Of course,' she agreed. 'A toast to success.'

His smile faded and he put his glass down on the table. 'That's the same thing you said to me the last time we were together,' he murmured, 'before I left for Central America. We were in Carmel at that little restaurant with the open fireplace... There were so many things I wanted to tell you that night...'

She felt the breath catch in her throat. 'What things?'

For an instant, his eyes held hers and she felt, more than saw, a lambent warmth in their depths, and then his glance slipped to the gold wedding-ring she still wore.

'Forget it,' he said, his face a clouded mask. 'It doesn't matter.'

'It does,' she said quickly, leaning towards him.

He lifted his glass and sipped at his wine. 'No, it doesn't,' he said flatly. 'We were two different people then. The girl I had dinner with that night was my fiancée. The woman across the table from me now is my brother's widow.'

'You make it sound like a ... a mathematical equation,' she said sharply, 'as if it were all neatly balanced and uncomplicated.'

'It is, isn't it? I went away, and you married Justin. It's as simple as that.'

'Nothing is ever as simple as that, Luke. Why do you keep trying to reduce things to black and white?'

'Caitlin,' he said carefully, 'I don't want to fight with you any more.'

'I don't either,' she said quickly. 'I just want us to talk about...'

He shook his head. 'Well, I don't,' he said firmly. 'There's no point.'

She paused while the waitress served their salads, weighing what she would say to him, feeling as if something she had almost had within her grasp were slipping away.

'Luke... you said you wanted to get on with your life. How can you possibly do that without understanding what happened?'

He leaned across the table towards her and his face darkened. 'Tell me something,' he said roughly. 'Can you say anything that will erase what's happened?'

'No, but...'

'That's all, then,' he said quickly. 'Let's not ruin lunch, Cat. The fact that we're sitting here, talking to each other, is more than I expected. So let's not lose ground. Tell me about something that we can handle. Tell me about Evian.'

It was useless to tell him what she was thinking, pointless to say please, before it's too late, let's talk about us. The last thing she wanted to do was spoil the fragile truce forming between them. With a sigh, Caitlin nodded her head and looked away from him.

'Of course. There's a lot you should know about the merger.'

She plunged immediately into a concise history of the French firm's proposal, trusting her mind to dispense pertinent facts even while part of her thoughts agonised over her foolishness in thinking that what he had felt when he saw the cinema poster was the same, quicksilver admission of love that had surged through her; the simple truth was that he'd probably felt nothing more than nostalgic regret. Yet even that was better than the rage and hatred he'd offered the other night.

His questions about Evian interrupted her, and as his comments and demands for facts became more specific, Caitlin found it necessary to concentrate all her attention on the information he wanted. Gradually, without willing it, they fell into an easy give-and-take of technical information, dropping back into their old habit of finishing each other's sentences, challenging each other when needed, using a kind of verbal shorthand that had developed between them years before. At some point between dessert and coffee, his comments became less frequent and she felt his eyes on her, but when she looked up, he dropped his glance to the table. Finally, as the waitress refilled her cup for the second time, she leaned back and sighed.

'Well, I think that's all of it, Luke. I can't think of anything I left out, unless you have some questions.'

'Lord, no,' he grinned. 'You know, I used to feel guilty about steering you away from studying biology, but now I think encouraging you to study business administration was the wisest move I ever made.'

'Well, thank you,' she murmured, blushing slightly. 'But you didn't turn me away from biology.'

'Sure I did, Cat. Your father talked me into giving you a job that summer you left school, remember? You said you wanted to work in the lab, that you were planning to be a biologist, and the very next day I found you sobbing into your coffee.'

A smile lit her face as she listened to him. 'I'd almost forgotten that,' she admitted. 'I'd spent the whole first day cleaning out guinea-pig cages, and I thought the poor little things were the test subjects in some gruesome experiment. Was I relieved when you told me they were part of a longevity study! The truth was, I probably only thought I wanted to be a biologist because my mother had been one. I suppose it had something to do with losing her when I was little. I wanted to be everything she had been,'

Luke raised his coffee cup in a toast and grinned at her. 'Whatever the reason, the world may have lost a biologist, but Thomas's gained one hell of a fine administrator.'

She blushed with pleasure at his praise, dismayed that it should be so important to her.

'I'm glad you're satisfied,' she said quietly.

'Satisfied?' He laughed aloud. 'You're terrific, Cat. Just the way you always were.' Impulsively, he reached across the table and covered her hand with his.

His touch and his words flushed her with a rush of sensation. She felt as if she were barely able to breathe, as if the hand he had touched was the only part of her body she could feel. He snatched his hand away and their eyes met. She knew she should say something, anything, but her brain and tongue seemed numb. Quickly, he turned away and signalled for their bill.

'Look,' he said hurriedly, busying himself with his wallet, 'there are still some bits and pieces of this Evian deal we should talk about, without any interference from Emily or Warren. If you have nothing planned for the rest of the day, I thought maybe we could just walk for a while. Unless you have something more important in mind...'

Caitlin fought back the tiny swell of excitement that trembled within her.

'That sounds like a good idea,' she said, trying to sound as casual as he did.

'Okay,' he said, almost gruffly. 'After all, if we're going to be working together, we might as well try and get along with each other.'

Her heart seemed to be thudding so loudly that she

feared he could hear it as he pulled back her chair and helped her to her feet.

'Oh, I agree,' she said quickly. 'And we have, haven't we? I mean, lunch went well just now. It . . .'

'It seemed like old times for a while,' he said quietly.

A bittersweet sorrow welled up within her and she nodded, acknowledging the truth of what he had said without trusting herself to answer aloud.

They left the restaurant and walked slowly along the Rue de Seine, heading away from the quick tempo of the broad boulevards. The street became more picturesque as they walked its length. Modern boutiques and offices gave way to older, handsome buildings tucked tightly against each other as they drew nearer to the river that wound through the heart of the city like a lazy serpent. For a long while, neither Caitlin nor Luke spoke; when finally they did, their comments were light exchanges about the cobblestoned street or the charming old houses. Caitlin's thoughts kept returning to that electric moment between them in the restaurant, trying to make sense of it, even as she warned herself that it had probably been meaningless, nothing more nor less than a careless gesture, a remnant of what they had once had. She never heard the sudden babble of childish voices ahead until a group of neatly uniformed children, their school bags trailing after them like the tails of kites, came barrelling unexpectedly around a corner.

'Look out,' Luke warned, laughing as he drew her out of the children's path. 'Even traffic on the pavements is dangerous in Paris.'

'It certainly is,' Caitlin gasped. 'Imagine trying to explain to a gendarme that you've been run over by a bunch of four-foot-high little kids! I don't think my French is good enough for that.'

'Well, mine surely isn't,' he said, smiling at her. 'Do you want to keep walking, or would you feel safer if I found a taxi?'

'No,' she said quickly, 'no, I'd love to walk a bit longer. We're almost at the river, aren't we? Would you like to cross it and walk along the other side?'

'That sounds good to me, Cat. Better stay close to me, though. Who knows if there are other packs of rampaging kids on the loose?'

He smiled down at her. His arm, which had remained protectively around her, dropped to his side and he took her hand and tucked it into the crook of his elbow. They continued walking towards the Seine, and it occurred to Caitlin that they looked the same as any other pair of tourists on this beautiful day.

Paris was wearing her brightest, most charming face. There was a crisp, cool tang of autumn in the air, but the trees still wore their summer greenery and the sun was warm and bright above them. From time to time, she glanced up at Luke as they walked, her face bright with a glow it had not had for a long time. The old, narrow streets that she had only recently had no urge to wander now seemed the most delightful pathways. Everything she saw—an *agent de police* directing traffic, a tiny art gallery, a dog sitting on a chair next to its master at a pavement café—seemed to be part of a painting by Renoir or Monet. Finally, they reached the river and began to cross the bridge to the other side.

Caitlin said, the words tumbling from her lips before she could stop them, 'That has to be the Louvre on the far bank. Do you think we have time to go there? We always planned . . .' Her voice faltered as the reality of their situation closed around her like a dark curtain. 'We had lots of plans, didn't we?' she murmured tonelessly.

Luke's footsteps slowed and he seemed to whisper his answer. 'Yes, Cat, I guess we did.'

'Luke, I'm sorry.' Her voice roughened with anger at herself. 'I don't know why I said that ... it just slipped out.'

He drew away from her and dug his hands deep into his pockets. 'It's okay,' he said carefully. 'Spending the afternoon together this way made me remember, too. I suppose it's impossible to forget the past entirely, even if you want to.'

She took a deep breath and looked up at him. 'Are you sure that's what you really want? To forget everything we had once?' Her words were rushed together, as if she were fearful of asking the question and even more fearful of hearing his answer.

They had reached the far side of the Seine and he paused and leaned against the railing of the bridge, staring down at the grey-green water surging beneath them.

'I don't really know what we had, Cat,' he said finally, in a voice so low it was almost a whisper. 'Everything seemed so clear to me a few days ago ... I thought I hated you the other night, but now ...'

Hesitantly, her hand reached out to touch him, but he moved away.

'I want to hate you, Cat,' he said almost angrily. 'But I can't, and I just don't understand it. I ... I feel as if I were lost in a maze of mirrors—I can't separate the false image from the true path out.'

'I can tell you what's true,' she said quickly. 'I can explain ...'

He swung around to face her with an expression that had hardened into bitterness.

'Explain what?' he asked brusquely. 'And whose

truth will you tell me, Cat? What image will I get this time?'

'Stop it,' she said sharply. Tears of anger and frustration slid down her cheeks. 'Stop it,' she repeated in an agonised whisper. 'I don't have to defend myself, Luke.' She inhaled deeply and tried to steady her voice before she continued. 'Why do you ... how can you just assume the worst about me?'

'Why are you still wearing his wedding-ring?' he countered, ignoring her question.

She looked down at the thin gold wedding-ring with surprise, so used to wearing it to keep men from asking her out that she had all but forgotten it.

'It's a simple question, Caitlin.'

She looked up at his sharp tone. Whatever faint warmth she thought she had seen in him earlier had vanished. He was looking at her, she thought suddenly, as if he had never seen her before, never loved her. An illusion, she thought bitterly—their entire day together had been nothing but an illusion, born out of his nostalgia and her weakness. With weary resignation, she turned away from him in defeat, not able to answer.

'Okay,' he said finally, 'I want my corporation, and you want the job with Clarke, I'll use my influence with my family and support you against the merger, and then you'll return my shares to me. No more bitter words, no more dredging up the past ... we can manage that, can't we?'

'Yes, I'm sure we can,' she said stiffly, surprised that she could even manage to say the words. 'We always were a good team, weren't we?'

Something seemed to darken in his eyes for the briefest tick of eternity, and then it was gone.

'The best,' he said at last, and he held out his hand to her.

'Yes,' she whispered, as she placed her hand in his, 'yes, we really were.'

With great formality, they shook hands and sealed their pact.

CHAPTER SIX

'I DON'T know why you refuse to move up the stockholders' meeting, Caitlin,' Emily Thomas said petulantly the next morning. She leaned over a tray of croissants and poked delicately at them with her finger. 'Isn't there any *pain au chocolat*? I most specifically asked for some.'

'There were two, Mother,' Warren said, adding sugar to his coffee. 'You've already eaten them both.'

'Well, it's not my fault that the French have such peculiar breakfast habits. You'd think they'd have learned something about the importance of the first meal of the day, wouldn't you?'

Caitlin sighed and turned to her secretary, who was sitting beside her with a non-committal look on her face. She felt tired, although the day had barely begun. The day spent with Luke had left her disturbed and uneasy, and it had been difficult to concentrate on the papers Jean had left in ther suite for today's meeting. She had managed only a few hours of troubled sleep and her patience with the self-centred Emily, never too good to start with, was at an all-time low. With great effort, she managed to speak calmly to Jean.

'Would you mind calling down for something more substantial for Aunt Emily, Jean?'

Jean nodded and got to her feet.

'Thank you,' Emily said frostily. 'I don't know why you insist we wait for Luke before we get started. You already know he agrees with me.'

'Yes, Caitlin, why the delay? He can't vote on this anyway.'

'I already explained that, Warren,' Caitlin said patiently. 'It's only right we hear his opinion. As for voting—we have to wait until the meeting. The others haven't arrived yet, and neither have their proxy votes. There's still time before the deadline, you know,' she added pointedly.

'They probably aren't going to show up, Caitlin. And some of them never bother sending in their proxies. I don't see why we should wait any longer; the major stockholders are all present, anyway.'

Caitlin uncrossed her legs and got up from her chair. 'Tell me, Warren,' she said pleasantly, 'would you be so eager to vote right now if you didn't have the proxies you and your mother need in your pocket?'

He flushed and tugged at his earlobe. 'Just because two of my cousins have agreed to support the merger . . .'

'Just because they have, you know you can carry the decision. But we have rules of procedure, Warren, and I refuse to circumvent them.'

'Nonsense, Caitlin,' Emily said immediately, a frown creasing her forehead. 'This is a family-owned corporation. We made the rules and we can change them.'

'Not prior to an announced meeting,' Caitlin said firmly. 'It's not good business practice, and I would think there's something in the by-laws to prevent it.'

'Can you substantiate that?' Warren demanded, and Caitlin began to rummage through the papers in her briefcase.

'I can,' Luke said from the doorway. Caitlin glanced up at him with a sigh of relief.

'Good morning,' she said quietly. 'We've been waiting for you.'

'I'm sorry, I was delayed. Good morning, everyone,' he added, crossing the room and sitting down opposite

Emily and her son. 'Warren, in answer to your question—when we first drew up our rules of procedure, we specifically drafted item nine to prevent just the kind of thing you're proposing.'

'Then I fail to see any point to this meeting,' Emily said, a sharp note of irritation creeping into her voice.

Luke smiled pleasantly at his aunt. 'Caitlin and I spent a lot of time at the Evian lab yesterday. It's only fitting that we tell you what we saw. You do have an open mind about this, don't you?'

Without waiting for an answer, he began to outline the details of their visit to Evian. Caitlin crossed the room and sat down beside him as he spoke. She listened in silence, handing him printouts and notes from her briefcase when necessary, only interrupting once or twice to add some additional information to his presentation. He would have little trouble handling his cousins when they arrived, she thought, pleased at the ease with which he'd absorbed the complicated material. It was almost as if no time had passed since he had been an active driving-force behind Thomas Pharmaceuticals. She was caught up in watching him, even while part of her was engrossed in mentally checking off his facts and figures. When, after half an hour, Warren began to chuckle softly she looked up in surprise.

'Did I miss something?' she asked softly, turning to face him.

'Yes, please, share it with all of us, Warren,' Luke added. 'I didn't realise I'd said something funny.'

'Oh, it's nothing you said. I simply suddenly thought of how amusing all this is. Mother and I would have bet our last dollar that you'd oppose Caitlin, wouldn't we, Mother? And yet, here you are, racing to support her position, championing her cause.' Warren shook his head and held up his hands.

'I didn't mean to interrupt, Luke, but...' He shrugged helplessly and began to smile. 'You must admit, it's a bit hard to accept.'

'I don't know why it should be,' Luke answered coolly. 'Her position is the right one for the company. If you'd just stop thinking about the short-term benefits of this merger and pay some attention to what I've been saying, you might even begin to admit it to yourself.'

Warren crossed the room and poured himself another cup of coffee. 'I'm not going to debate my attitude with you, Luke. I think my mother and I have already made our positions perfectly clear. What I was referring to was the admirable ease with which dear Caitlin seems to win over whichever Thomas brother she needs at a given moment. No offence, Caitlin,' he drawled. 'Still, you must admit it's rather droll.'

'I won't play your game, Warren,' she answered. 'We're here to talk about Thomas Pharmaceuticals and nothing other than that.'

'Caitlin's absolutely right...' Luke began and Warren burst out laughing.

'And isn't that an all-too-familiar phrase? I seem to remember hearing it years ago, Luke, and from you, if memory serves, when she barely had the right to attend these family functions.'

Caitlin's face whitened with anger. 'I certainly did have the right,' she said quickly. 'I had my own shares...'

'For heaven's sake, Caitlin, don't bring up your miserable little five percent again, please,' Emily interrupted.

'Yes, do spare us that. I'd much rather you talked about the marvellous technique you seem to have, my dear.' Warren set his cup and saucer down and smiled unpleasantly. 'You must tell us some time how you used it to persuade Evian to offer you stock options once they knew you opposed the merger. Did she tell you that, Luke? How she spent an evening with the chairman of their board and how he fattened his offer for her personally?'

Luke got to his feet and took a step towards his cousin.

'Why don't you ask her?' Warren said quickly, moving towards his mother. 'Matter of fact, why don't you ask her if that's why she's so opposed to the deal? Perhaps she's holding out for an even bigger piece of the action.'

Caitlin snatched up her briefcase and stuffed her papers into it. 'I will not preside over this ... this brawl,' she said coldly. 'This meeting is adjourned.'

She pivoted on her heel and stalked from the room. Behind her, she heard Emily's outraged cry and Luke's voice rising in anger, but she didn't look back, not even when she heard him call her name. She was halfway down the corridor when he caught up to her and grasped her shoulder.

'It isn't true, is it?'

'How can you even ask me that?' she demanded bitterly, pulling free of him. 'I told Evian I didn't want their stock. This whole deal is a fraud.'

'Those options would be worth a lot of money, Cat. But I suppose this job with Clarke is worth even more to you.'

'Yes, it is,' she said stiffly, wincing inwardly at the lie.

'Okay,' Luke said slowly, 'okay, I believe you.'

'Thank you for nothing,' she said through her teeth. 'Am I supposed to be grateful for that vote of confidence? The other job has nothing to do with this, Luke. As long as I'm with Thomas, I'll be loyal to it. I only want what's best for this firm. But Warren only wants what's best for his wallet. That's all there is to it, and if you think I'm going to just sit back and listen to his horrible accusations, or try and defend myself to all of you...' Without warning, tears sprang to her eyes. 'Just let me alone, will you? Go back in there and just finish talking to your family.'

'I've already finished,' he said roughly, taking her arm and ringing for the lift. 'I told Warren what would happen to him the next time he decided to run off at the mouth. Emily is probably patting his hand this minute and promising to protect him from me.' He grinned at her as the lift door opened. 'She told me she'd never heard such language in her life, but I bet that won't stop her from tucking into her breakfast when it gets there. Here,' he added gruffly, handing her his handkerchief, 'dry your eyes. You don't want to spoil that executive image of yours, do you?'

Caitlin smiled and dabbed at her eyes. 'I don't feel much like an executive this minute. I don't know why I let those two get under my skin that way.'

'Actually, I thought you did rather well, considering the job Warren was trying to do on you.'

'I wasn't prepared for that kind of attack.' Carefully, she folded the handkerchief and handed it back. 'I guess what really pushed him over the edge was your support of my position.'

Luke shrugged and smiled at her. 'You were more than holding your own with him. I have to admit, I got a kick out of seeing him on the defensive with you.'

Caitlin looked at him and smiled as they stepped out into the hotel corridor and started towards her suite. 'That's a charitable description of what happened, don't you think? He wanted to chew me into little pieces, Luke.'

'Only because he felt trapped, Cat. He knew you

had the facts, and that's why he tried to hit you with those low blows. But you handled him like a pro.'

She unlocked the door to her suite and turned to face him. 'Well,' she said, smiling slightly, 'I feel better now. Why don't you wait a minute while I splash some cold water on my face, and then we'll go back and beard the lions in their den?' Her smile widened and she began to laugh. 'Come to think of it, after all that talk of proper procedure, I don't think I had the legal right to adjourn that meeting the way I did.'

'Extraordinary circumstances,' he said innocently, and then he laughed. 'Well, if it's not in the by-laws, it should be. No, let them cool their heels a while, Cat. I don't think we have anything more to say to them just now, anyway. Suppose I call down for some coffee while you freshen up? Unless ... would you rather I left?'

She shook her head. 'No, a cup of coffee would be terrific. I won't be a minute ...' She hurried into the bathroom, hoping the complexity of emotions she felt didn't show on her face. 'Don't be a fool, Caitlin,' she whispered to herself furiously as she splashed cool water on her eyes and then wiped off the last traces of fading mascara. 'Nothing has changed ... he's just pleased with how things went with Emily and Warren.'

Yet, when she returned to the sitting room, her heart seemed to leap at the sight of his smiling face.

'Coffee will be here in a minute. I was half tempted to order champagne, but I thought even the French might raise their eyebrows if I asked for it at this hour of the morning.'

Caitlin smiled. 'Haven't they ever heard of a champagne brunch? Anyway, coffee's more in line with the way I feel.'

There was a discreet knock at the door and she opened it to admit a waiter wheeling a linen-covered table on which gleamed a silver coffee service and delicate Limoges cups and saucers. He bowed and then set about placing the table before the sunny windows, arranging white damask napkins at each place-setting before carefully drawing up two chairs. Caitlin cleared her throat and turned away as the waiter stepped back from his handiwork and nodded solemnly.

'Très bien, garçon. Merci,' she said when he turned to her for approval. Once the door had safely closed behind him, she turned to Luke and smiled. 'This is a long way from the office, isn't it? I'm used to having my morning coffee from a chipped mug with a picture of Snoopy on it.'

'I can't imagine that, Cat.'

Caitlin poured coffee for both of them and smiled. 'That's the real me,' she admitted. 'I suspect Emily feels more comfortable in this kind of setting than I do.'

'Oh, I don't know, Cat. You seemed very much at home in that conference room.'

She smiled and sipped at her coffee. 'That's because I feel at home dealing with facts, figures, the business details of the corporation. But all this . . .' she gestured at the room and its elegant appointments, 'has nothing to do with me. Does that make sense?'

Luke pulled his chair closer to the table. 'Yes, I feel the same way. This is so far removed from the reality of the lab and the office . . . But this is Emily's reality. She only sees Thomas's as a money machine. Profitable, but not as lucrative as the merger.'

Caitlin looked up at him and smiled. 'Well, you may not have changed her mind, but at least you've given Warren something to think about.'

'Yes, he did look terrified, didn't he?' Luke leaned back in his chair and chuckled. 'I suppose I always wanted to take him on, but I never had the chance before. In the past, I was always able to swing enough of the others so Warren knew it wouldn't pay to fight it out.'

Caitlin looked at him appraisingly. 'You almost sound as if you're looking forward to this.'

'I don't know,' he said thoughtfully, 'maybe I am. I still wouldn't say a boardroom skirmish is as exciting as hiking over a mountain ridge or sailing through a squall . . .'

'Or discovering a new vaccine,' she added, and he smiled with a charming honesty.

'Definitely not in that league, no. But it's going to be fun. I used to think that part of the business was just time wasted away from the lab—necessary, but not terrific—but I found I missed it, these past few years.'

Caitlin returned his smile. 'You mean you won't have to be shanghaied into attending meetings from now on? That's hard to believe.'

'Well,' he admitted, 'I'll probably always prefer a test tube to an annual report, but you can't expect miracles, can you?'

'Speaking of miracles, I'd have thought Emily would have tracked us down by now. I wonder if . . .' She started as the shrill ring of the telephone interrupted her. 'I bet I know who that is,' she murmured, lifting the receiver. 'Hello?' She nodded at Luke and rolled her eyes upward. 'Yes, Emily. Yes, I know. No, not yet. Yes, I shall. Yes, yes, later.' She hung up the phone and sighed. 'Emily wants to know if I've heard from any of your cousins yet. I think she's afraid I'm going to hit them over the head and steal their proxies as they appear.'

'Not a bad idea,' Luke chuckled. 'Although I don't think we'll have to go that far to convince them. Actually, it might be enough just to let them talk to you.'

'To me?' she repeated in surprise.

'Sure. You're the one who discovered the problem with Evian, not me.'

'That's only because I had the facts. No, thanks for the kind words, but talking to me won't do it. I think Emily has been stirring them up for a while now. She keeps hinting that they're going to catch me in some sort of error, sooner or later. In some ways, she's pretty old-fashioned, you know. I suspect she's not comfortable with decisions made by me because I'm a woman.'

'A beautiful woman,' Luke said softly. 'That's a potent combination, you know. Beauty and intelligence . . . those are assets you can't list on a balance sheet.'

Their eyes met across the table and Caitlin's heartbeat quickened at the frank admiration she saw reflected in his gaze.

'That was something special you always had, Cat. It's more apparent now than ever.'

She cast about for some sort of response, but none seemed appropriate. He had caught her off guard again, not only with his compliments but with the same flicker of warmth he'd shown the day before. He smiled and his hand moved towards hers where it lay on the white tablecloth, and she drew in her breath as his fingers grazed her wrist.

The fragile moment between them was shattered by the intrusive cry of the telephone. Luke pulled his hand back and got to his feet. Caitlin watched as he shoved his hands deep into his pockets and stared out of the window. Finally, on the fourth ring, she snatched at the phone.

'Yes, what is it?' she said sharply, her eyes still on Luke. 'Emily, I told you . . . yes, I said that I would. No, please don't. There's no need for that, Emily. Emily?' She slammed down the phone and Luke turned and faced her.

'Trouble?' he asked calmly.

'No, not really,' she said slowly. 'Emily wants to come up here and join us. I . . . asked her not to. I didn't think we'd get much work done with her breathing over our shoulders,' she added hastily, afraid he would sense that the truth was more complex than that. 'I could phone down and ask the concierge to hold my calls . . .'

'That won't stop Emily—and we're never going to get our strategy organised if we spend all our time dodging her.' He smiled suddenly and snapped his fingers. 'Look, I've got a great idea. It's a beautiful day out. Why don't we clear our heads a little, get out into the air for a couple of hours, and avoid my aunt all at the same time?'

Caitlin shook her head doubtfully. 'I don't know, Luke. I'm not sure we should.'

'Come on, Cat. Your secretary can take any calls that come in, if that's what's worrying you. We can't play hide and seek with Emily all morning, can we?'

'We couldn't leave even if we wanted to,' she said slowly. 'Knowing your aunt, she's probably going to be knocking at the door in about two minutes, even though I told her not to.'

'Then we don't have a second to waste, do we? Come on, woman, get a move on.'

Luke grabbed Caitlin's hand and pulled her to her feet.

'This is crazy,' she said, hurrying along with him to the door. 'I've got to at least tell Jean that I'm leaving . . .'

'You can leave word at the desk. Hurry, Cat,' he urged, as she paused to snatch up her jacket. 'You don't want to open that door and stumble into Emily, do you?'

'But where are we going?' she whispered, as they rushed down the corridor.

'To a place where they won't be able to find us, where we can do some serious thinking.'

'Are you certain?'

A teasing smile lit his face. 'Are you doubting the wisdom of my first executive decision in almost four years?'

She smiled at him in return and shook her head, wordlessly following him into the lift, conscious of nothing but the warm pressure of his hand on hers.

CHAPTER SEVEN

LUKE refused to tell her where they were going, offering her only the right to choose between getting there by Metro or by taxi.

'The Metro, by all means,' Caitlin said immediately. 'I haven't been in it since we got to Paris.'

She saw an electric map as soon as they entered the underground station and hoped he'd use it so that she might learn their mysterious destination, but he seemed to know their route beforehand and whisked her through the turnstile and on to the platform without any hesitation. Even while Caitlin chastised herself for agreeing to leave the hotel with him, she felt drawn to share in the feeling that they were conspirators eluding the enemy. She warned herself not to be fooled by Luke's relaxed, carefree mood. It was business that had brought them together; in the past, they'd done some of their best planning for Thomas's while walking along the beach or through the park.

She glanced up at him as the train pulled into the station. Yes, that was what all this must be about. The hotel suite, elegant as it was, was stuffy and confining. He'd probably found a quiet, green corner in a park somewhere, with a bench to sit on, where they could plot their next moves without interruption.

They entered the train and she looked around her with curiosity. The carriage was similar to others she'd ridden in, in San Francisco, or London, or New York, but it was impossible not to be charmed by the variety of languages she heard or the colourful advertisements. Her glance fell upon a route map. Smiling to herself, she read the names of the stations they would pass, recognising some of them from books and films, until she reached one that made her pause.

'Les Buttes Chaumont?' she said aloud. 'Is that where we're going?' she asked in surprise.

Luke nodded and leaned towards her. 'That's the place,' he admitted. 'You don't mind, do you? I've always wanted to see it.'

'Yes, I know,' she murmured. 'I remember. It's the park where they say children go to sail their model boats. You used to joke that it was probably the only place you could race a sailing boat and win.'

'You really don't mind going there, do you, Cat?' he asked quickly. 'I just thought it would probably be pretty quiet on a weekday afternoon, and we can get some work done while we walk.'

'It's fine with me, Luke,' she said after a slight hesitation.

He gave her a faint smile and she managed to return it before looking away from him. Paris had other parks, she thought in confusion. There was the flower-lined walk through the Tuileries and the Champs de Mars and the Bois de Boulogne ... why had he chosen this less known, less convenient one? Why would he want them to go to a place they'd talked about, years before, joked about the day he'd lost a race off the California coast at Santa Barbara?

'The first thing we'll do when we get to Paris,' he'd said while she'd tried unsuccessfully not to laugh at the sight of him with strands of seaweed trailing from his hair, 'is buy a model sailing boat and take it to the lake at Les Buttes Chaumont.'

'Good idea,' she'd said solemnly. 'I'm sure you can win against ten-year-old competitors.'

'You'll pay for that unkind remark, young woman,'

he'd said quickly. 'Just for being so cruel, sailing the boat will be the second thing we do in Paris.'

And then they had both started to laugh, and he'd caught her in his arms and kissed her. She could still remember the wet, wonderful feel of his body against hers, the salt-tanged scent of him, the feeling that the future ahead of them was infinite and glorious.

As Luke had predicted, the park was all but deserted. There were a few dedicated joggers along the pathway as they entered and several young women pushing prams, but once they had walked further, Caitlin was struck by a sense of quiet and serenity.

'How peaceful it is here,' she said, trying to keep up with Luke's long strides.

He agreed, smiling at her. 'We'll find a spot down there, by the lake, and . . . Cat, look. There's a boat out on the water. A nice looking one, at that. Would you mind . . . it will just take a minute . . .'

She smiled at him and nodded her head.

Ahead of them, a small boy knelt patiently on the grassy shore of the sun-dappled lake as a large model boat, its sails filled by a gentle breeze, cut through the water towards him. Caitlin and Luke stopped a few feet away and watched as the ship knifed gracefully towards the child's outstretched hands.

'Good-looking model, son,' Luke said, and the boy looked up and frowned.

'Pardon, monsieur?'

Luke cleared his throat and smiled self-consciously. 'I said, uh, *le . . . le bateau, uh, il est bien, uh, bon . . .* Cat,' he whispered anxiously, 'how do I tell the kid that I like his model?'

'I think you'd better worry about how you tell his mother that you're not a child molester,' she murmured, leaning closer to him. 'That woman sitting on the bench over there is looking at us strangely.'

Luke glanced over his shoulder. '*Bonjour, madame,*' he called and then he bent his head to Caitlin's. 'She looks as if she thinks I'm a murderer,' he muttered. 'All I'd like to do is try the boat . . .'

He leaned down as the boat nudged into the shoreline and smiled at the little boy. 'May I?' he asked, gesturing at the model. 'I, uh, *je* . . . Cat, please, tell him I like sailing, and ask him if . . .'

'Would you care to sail it, *monsieur*?' the child asked suddenly in perfect, charmingly accented English.

Luke nodded happily and knelt beside him, 'May I? Just once?'

The child stared at him solemnly. 'Certainly, *monsieur*. I would be honoured.'

Carefully, he relinquished the hull and, with great ceremony, Luke angled the boat into the wind and pushed it off. Caitlin smiled as she watched the man and the boy exchange satisfied glances as the little ship heeled on its side and sped across the lake.

Luke's face was relaxed and contented, and yet there was a difference about it, a shadowed presence in his eyes, that filled Caitlin with a sudden ache. He and the child were laughing together, watching as the boat cut in front of a sleepy, startled duck, and Caitlin blinked back the sudden pressure of tears in her eyes. She felt almost overcome by the urge to bend down and put her arms around him, and she shoved her hands into her jacket pockets as if they might betray her. Deliberately, she turned away from the lake and met the irritated stare of the woman stalking towards them.

'Luke,' Caitlin said quickly, 'I think it's about time we left.'

He looked up in surprise and then rose to his feet. 'Yes, of course. Uh, you have a charming little boy, *madame*,' he said hurriedly as the woman brushed past them and took the child by the hand.

'*Au revoir, mon ami*,' the boy called, as she whisked him along the path leading around the lake. 'Perhaps we can play together another time, yes?'

Caitlin burst out laughing as the woman bent down and chattered angrily at the child.

'Well, you win some and you lose some,' she said. 'At least he liked you.'

'That's because I feel like a kid myself this minute,' Luke grinned as they walked away from the shoreline.

Caitlin agreed. 'After all, only a pair of juveniles would be here in the middle of the day instead of being at work.'

They followed the path as it began a swing upwards. The buttes for which the park was named surrounded them like the rocky sides of a great bowl. Gradually, as the path steepened, Caitlin's footsteps slowed.

'From the sound of all that huffing and puffing you're doing, you've been locked away at a desk too long. What's the matter, Cat? Don't tell me this little hill is too difficult for you.'

'Little hill?' she repeated indignantly. 'Is that what you call this . . . this track for mountain goats?'

'You can do it,' he insisted. 'Just put your mind to it.'

'My mind isn't the problem,' she gasped as the path steepened. 'It's these awful high heels . . .'

'A feeble excuse,' he said tauntingly. 'You're just out of shape.'

Caitlin shook her head and took several ragged breaths. 'Not so,' she finally managed. 'I took up jogging a while ago. But trotting along a flat, paved road in sneakers isn't the same as . . . Luke, please,' she groaned, 'give me a minute to get my wind back.'

He laughed and dropped to the grass beside the path. 'Okay, weakling, you've got sixty seconds. So you took up the great California sport, hmm?' She nodded her head and he smiled. 'So did I. Really,' he insisted when she frowned in disbelief. 'That was how I kept in shape, once they began to let me out of the hut. I used to jog around the village, leaping over squawking chickens, scattering frightened burros, while the little kids pointed at me and laughed.'

'They didn't try and stop you?'

'Stop me?' He laughed again, and it was such an infectious sound that she began to smile even before he spoke. 'Listen, I was their only entertainment. The crazy gringo, shirt tails flapping, trying to avoid the piles of donkey dung, not always successfully, I might add, was better than anything they had going for them. And it was a great feeling. I can't describe it, but on really good days, when I was running just right, my mind would kind of float free. It's impossible to explain, but . . .'

'But suddenly you would be elsewhere, looking down on yourself, seeing colours you'd never seen, hearing every bird call as if for the first time.'

Luke looked at her in surprise. 'Yes, that's it exactly. It was almost as if I wasn't there in that ugly place any more.'

Caitlin sighed and plucked a blade of grass from beside her. 'Yes, I know that feeling. That's how it is for me when I run. I started it for the physical part, to get in shape after the long hours just sitting at my desk, but then it became something else, a place to lose myself, to get away from all the things pressing in on me . . .' Her words faded into silence and she looked up and smiled apologetically. 'Sorry. I didn't mean to make it sound like a mystical experience.'

'Don't apologise, Cat.' His eyes narrowed and he glanced away from her. 'Sometimes, when I was running, I'd find my thoughts in the craziest places.'

'My thoughts were of you,' she said simply, not

daring to look at him. 'I used to remember things we did together, places we went...'

A soft breeze sighed through the trees, and Luke stirred beside her.

'Maybe it was mental telepathy,' he said softly. 'Sometimes, I could almost see your face before me, smiling, looking as if nothing mattered in the whole world except for us...'

Her heart lurched within her. 'Luke...'

He scrambled to his feet. 'Come on,' he said gruffly. 'You've had more than your sixty seconds.'

Caitlin stood up slowly, regretting her admission to him, cursing the obstinacy that kept making her try and push him towards something unattainable.

'Maybe we should go back down,' she said after a few minutes had dragged by in silence. 'There were some benches near the lake...'

'Not when we're so near the top,' he said brusquely. 'Can't you make it?'

'It's not that,' she began, but he reached out and grabbed hold of her hand.

'Just hang on to me,' he said, not looking at her. 'There isn't far to go.'

His touch seemed dry and impersonal, and she clung to him obediently, trudging along behind him as the path became a narrow trail cut into the side of the butte. She glanced to her left and peered downward. Below them, the lake glistened brightly in the late morning sun. As she watched, a flock of birds swooped low and settled like dark leaves on the grass beneath trees touched with colour or by the cool spring nights. Only the tall buildings on the horizon were a reminder that they were still in Paris.

Caitlin ducked her head as she followed Luke into a dark, cave-like opening in the side of the butte and then up a series of rough steps cut into the rocky slope. They had reached the end of the narrow trail. The park was far below them, a child's storybook view of trees and pathways, with the lake a tiny, glistening droplet at its heart. The wind, stronger than it had been at the bottom of the butte, caught her hair and teased it into a halo of soft curls.

'We're at the top of the world,' she said softly. 'How beautiful it is, Luke. I feel as if we're the only people left in the whole world.'

'You said that the day we climbed down to that hidden cove at Big Sur, Cat,' he said in a muted voice.

The caress of the wind and the intensity of the memory brought a splash of crimson to her cheeks.

'I remember,' she whispered.

'You said the world belonged to us, Cat, that lovers own a world no one else can share.' His hand tightened on hers and his voice roughened. 'Did you mean it?'

'You know that I did,' she murmured.

'Then why?' he demanded. 'Why Justin? If the world belonged to us? And why so soon? Didn't you even look back? What happened to all the promises we made to each other?'

'I never forgot any of them, Luke.'

'Or were they just empty words, Cat?' His eyes bored into hers and his words slurred together roughly. 'Is that it?'

'You know they weren't,' she said angrily, pulling free of him.

'I don't know a damned thing,' he growled, 'especially about you.'

'I've had enough of this,' she said, starting to step past him. 'I was a fool to come here with you. You said we could get along with each other, work together ... but you lied, didn't you?'

He moved past her quickly, blocking the narrow

pathway. 'Don't talk to me about lies, Cat. You're the expert in that field.'

Caitlin's face reddened with fury. 'Damn you! I never lied. You want to fit me into some neat little category you set up, label me, classify me . . .'

'Oh, how I wish I could,' he said bitterly. 'Then, at least, I'd know if it was me you'd wanted, or my brother, or only a foolproof way to get where you are today.'

'I'm going back to the hotel,' she snapped.

'You're not going anywhere until this is finished, Cat.'

There was the sudden sting of tears in her eyes as she looked at him. 'It is finished,' she said quickly. 'I know that now. You don't want to listen to the truth.'

He bent his head towards her and she drew back from the wild, heated look in his eyes.

'I asked you a question about that day at Big Sur. Was all that an act?'

Without warning, his arms closed around her. She gasped as his hands spread across her back, drawing her body tightly against his, and her hands flattened against his chest as she tried to pull free of his rough embrace.

'Stop it!' she said angrily. 'You have no right to treat me this way.'

She twisted her head to the side, but his mouth closed on hers without pity, his lips warm and hard against her wind-chilled flesh. For the briefest of seconds, time seemed an eternity as she struggled against him. Outrage at his attempt to pervert an act that had once joined them in love flooded through her, and then suddenly it was gone. Like a tidal wave ripping free of the ocean, all her pent-up longing and love for him erupted, and she threw her arms around his neck, gentling his mouth with hers, forcing the harshness of his kiss to change, to become the sweet fire she'd never forgotten. She pressed closer to him, desperately wanting to erase all his doubts and anger with the touch of her body, all her pain with the flood of emotions his kiss had unleashed.

He pulled free of her suddenly, his face so pale that his eyes seemed like dark stones within it.

'What are you trying to do to me?' he asked in a choked whisper. 'I already said you were a good actress. You don't have to do this to prove it.'

It was too late for her to draw back from the razor's edge on which she was balanced. Too many years of wanting him, too many dreams of being in his arms, were propelling her forward. It was as if the past few days had been leading inexorably to this single moment, and she could no longer prevent what she must finally admit.

'Don't say anything more to hurt me, Luke,' she begged, tears streaming down her face. 'I love you . . . I never loved anyone else. I tried to tell you the other night, but you wouldn't listen . . .'

'Stop it,' he said roughly. 'I don't believe you, Cat.'

'You must,' she said desperately. 'It's true, Luke. I love you.'

'It doesn't matter,' he murmured. 'I don't feel anything for you, Caitlin. Not any more.'

'No,' she cried.

'It's finished,' he insisted. 'It . . .' Suddenly, he reached out and took her by the shoulders, his fingers tightening on her until she felt their imprint would be branded into her flesh for ever. 'Oh, Caitlin,' he whispered, and all at once she felt the tension draining from his body, saw something springing to life in the darkness of his eyes, and then his mouth was on hers, warm and sweet and wonderful, his kiss telling her more than words ever could that he loved her, that the terrible years they had been apart were over at last, that all her empty, endless days and nights were done with.

'Caitlin, Caitlin,' he sighed, the softly murmured name a warm breath against her lips, 'I love you. I can't lie to you—to myself—any longer. Don't cry, darling,' he said softly, brushing his mouth against her damp cheek. 'Please, don't cry any more.' His hands caught in the silken, wind-tossed tangle of her hair as he lifted her face to his. 'Do you understand, Cat? I love you.'

Her hands moved across his shoulders, touched his face, as if she sought to convince herself that he was really there, in her arms, that this was not merely another dream from which she would awaken to cold, numbing reality. But no dream had ever been like this, she knew, as she felt the faint roughness of his cheek against hers.

'Luke,' she whispered, 'I've been so unhappy, so lonely . . . The other night . . .'

'Hush, Cat,' he said, cradling her in his arms. 'Those were two other people, darling, not us.'

'I thought you'd forgotten how it was between us, the way we loved each other . . .'

'I never forgot anything about you,' he said huskily. 'Not the way you look, or the way you feel, or the taste of your mouth, like honey and wildflowers and . . .'

His words were lost in the passion of their kiss. Caitlin sighed and gave herself up to the miracle of what was happening, while time and space whirled around her, carrying her back to the languid serenity that had held them safe that long-ago afternoon at Big Sur. At last, she leaned back against his encircling arms and raised her eyes to his.

'I have so much to tell you,' she said softly, 'so many things I want you to know, to understand . . .'

His arms tightened around her. 'Later,' he murmured. His hands slipped under her jacket, their warmth burning through her silk blouse. 'I don't want to do anything right now except kiss you, touch you...'

His mouth covered hers again and she pushed aside the shadowed thoughts that moved like phantom dancers through her mind. Nothing mattered except this, she thought, as a wild exultation surged through her.

A giggle and a wind-borne whisper drew her back to reality, and she opened her eyes and looked over his shoulder. Two wide-eyes children stared at her from the base of the rocky steps leading up from the cave-like opening in the butte.

'Luke—we have an audience,' she whispered.

He turned and groaned softly as he saw the pair of grinning urchins.

'*Bonjour*,' he said with forced amiability. '*Vous parlez anglais?*'

The children looked at each other and giggled.

'*Non, monsieur*,' said the tallest.

'That's fine,' Luke said, grinning at them. 'Why aren't you monsters in school? How'd you like me to report you to the truant officer?'

'Luke, that's terrible,' Caitlin hissed, trying not to laugh. 'Just smile at them nicely—is that the best you can do?—that's it, smile, don't scowl, and maybe they'll leave.'

'Don't be silly, Cat. I bet we're more fun to watch than anything else they can find around here. Come on,' he sighed, taking her hand in his, 'let's find a place with a little more privacy.'

She flashed an embarrassed smile at the children as she hurried after Luke, her high heels tapping a staccato beat on the rocks as she tried to keep up with him.

'Could you please slow down a little?' she asked breathlessly as the path widened. 'I'm delighted to know you want to rush me off so we can be alone, but if I break my ankle, we'll end up going crazy trying to make ourselves understood in a French hospital.'

He turned to her and smiled. 'Thomas men always rush off with their women,' he said.

The laugher and happiness that had filled her died instantly, as if a spectre had clamped a hand to her throat. She stared at him in silence, unable to speak a word.

'Cat, I didn't mean that the way it sounded,' he said quickly, drawing her to him and burying his face in her hair.

'Didn't you?' she whispered, pulling back to face him. 'Was that what you were really thinking? That Justin and I . . .'

He shook his head. 'No,' he insisted, 'no, I . . . Please, Cat, don't look at me that way,' he said, misery etched into his face. 'It just slipped out. It'll pass, darling. It will, you'll see.'

'It won't,' she murmured. 'That's why we have to talk, Luke. You must understand . . . I have to tell you everything.'

He touched his lips to her forehead. 'Not just yet, darling. It's too soon. I told you, the past is over.'

'But we're part of that past,' she insisted. 'We can't brush it aside, not if we want to begin again and build something good between us.'

'We have something good between us, Cat. That's the only part of the past we need to remember.'

She stepped closer to him and put her hand on his cheek. 'Luke' she whispered, 'I couldn't bear to have anything separate us again.'

He covered her hand with his and brought it to his mouth. 'Nothing will,' he promised softly.

Caitlin searched his eyes with hers. The sincerity of his pledge was plainly written in their warm glow. Still, a persistent fear, prompted by the still-fresh memory of how close they had come to losing each other, spurred her on.

'I know you mean that,' she said. 'I just want to make sure we bury all our old ghosts, so they can't rise up to haunt us again.'

He looked at her for a second, and then he reached out and gently tucked a strand of her hair behind her ear.

'Listen to me, Cat,' he said quietly. 'The simple truth is that I'm not ready to hear about you and Justin. I don't know if I'll ever be ready. Even if you had a thousand good reasons for marrying him . . .'

'One reason,' she interrupted.

'Even one good reason is more than I'm ready for. I just can't get past the fact that he . . . that you . . . my girl and my brother . . .' His voice broke and faded away into the silence. 'The truth doesn't always set you free,' he said. 'Sometimes, the weight of it is more than a person can bear.'

His eyes seemed to plead with hers for understanding. She thought of Justin, of his arrogant cruelty, and suddenly it seemed clear that the knowledge she held within her, this truth that she wanted to force upon the man she loved with all her heart, might indeed be a burden he could not bear in these first few days of his freedom. She looked at the lines etched alongside his mouth as if by a cruel sculptor and, hesitantly, she ran her finger along the scar on his cheek.

'You never did tell me how that happened.'

A muscle in his jaw tensed and his eyes seemed to darken and look into the past.

'It's nothing,' he said tightly. 'Just a souvenir of the welcoming party they threw for me after I was captured.'

Caitlin shuddered. 'It must have been terrible,' she whispered.

'It wasn't too terrific,' he said, and then his mouth softened and a faint smile lit his face. 'This day, this moment with you, is the first good thing that's happened to me in years. Let's not spoil it, please.'

She moved towards him, into his open arms, and with a sigh she leaned her head against his shoulder.

'I love you so much, Luke,' she murmured. 'I just want us to be happy.'

He tilted her face up to his and his lips brushed hers. 'We have each other again, Cat. When did we ever need more than that to be happy?'

It was such a basic truth that she could find no way to refute it. Her lips parted beneath his and his arms tightened around her, until the heat of the sun and the warmth of his embrace became one.

CHAPTER EIGHT

'THERE you are,' Jean said, breathing a sigh of relief as Caitlin stepped from the hotel lift. 'I've just about run out of excuses for you. Emily and her son have been poking into corners trying to find you.' She paused and gave Caitlin a suspicious look. 'Where have you been all day, anyway?'

'Wouln't you love to know?' Caitlin said mysteriously, winking at her secretary. She burst into delighted laughter at the surprised expression on Jean's face and tapped her lightly on the arm. 'Come on into my suite with me, and maybe I'll tell you.'

Caitlin unlocked the door and fairly danced into the sitting room, tossing her jacket and clutch bag carelessly on to a chair, kicking off her shoes as she padded to the window.

'What a perfectly glorious day,' she said, flinging open the curtains. 'Just look at that view—have you ever seen a city quite like Paris?'

Jean was methodically picking up Caitlin's discarded clothing and carrying it into the adjoining bedroom. 'What happened to you? You sound as if you spent the last eight hours at a pavement café, overdosing on Pernod.'

'Don't be such a cynic, Jean,' Caitlin laughed, whirling around to face her. 'What else is Paris famous for, besides Pernod and pavement cafés? Love, my friend.'

Her secretary trotted back into the sitting room and sank down on a chair. 'I'm supposed to believe you've met Prince Charming, is that right?' she asked, staring at Caitlin. 'Okay, don't tell me. Let me guess. Uh, you went to the Louvre and fell head over heels in love with a penniless young artist. Better still, you finally called the Marquis and he swept you off your feet. Not warm yet?' she said, when Caitlin started to shake her head and smile. 'I've got it this time. Knowing you, you probably felt sorry for some guinea-pig or white rat at the Evian lab and you called the RSPCA and the guy they sent over to investigate turned out to be Paul Newman in disguise. No?'

'Is it really so difficult to picture me in love with someone?'

'Not difficult, exactly. Just highly improbable. Still, it's an interesting possibility. I've got to admit, in all the time I've been working for you, I've never seen you look so ... so ...'

'So glowing? Happy? Ecstatic?'

'So smug,' Jean said flatly. 'Well, are you going to tell me what's going on? You might at least have warned me that you'd be doing a disappearing act.'

'I'm sorry, Jean. I didn't plan on it, believe me.' Caitlin smiled and collapsed on the couch opposite the other woman. 'Do you remember the other night, when I told you I'd dreamed of coming to Paris long ago? And you asked me who I'd planned the trip with? You said that nobody ...'

'Dreams about Paris alone,' Jean said impatiently. 'You told me more about yourself in that one little speech than I can ever recall hearing before.'

'The man I wanted to make that trip with is here. I spent the whole day with him,' Caitlin said happily, excitement shining in her eyes. 'And he still feels the same way about me, that's the most wonderful part. I knew I never stopped loving him, but the miracle is that he still loves me, too.'

Impulsively, Jean reached across to Caitlin and

clasped both her hands in hers. 'Oh, Caitlin, that's incredible. I'm so happy for you. You mean to say that this man just turned up, some time since you left here this morning, and told you he loves you?'

Caitlin shook her head and laughed. 'No, no. He turned up a couple of nights ago, right here in this very room . . .'

Jean sat back and stared at Caitlin through narrowed eyes. 'Hold it a minute,' she said carefully. 'Do you mean that Luke Thomas . . . that he's the one you . . .'

The smile vanished from Caitlin's face and she raised her chin defensively. 'I know how it sounds. But we were in love long before he vanished. And there's no reason to get that look on your face, either. I had good reasons for marrying his brother.'

'I'm sure you did, Caitlin. I'm not judging you. I've heard enough gossip around the office to realise the whole thing was complicated.' She flushed slightly and looked down at her lap.

Caitlin smiled and patted her secretary's arm. 'Trust me, Jean. I know what I'm doing.'

'You're the boss, Caitlin. Just keep in mind that directing a business isn't quite the same as directing your heart.'

'I know that. For one thing, I won't have the benefit of you running interference for me.' A smile tugged at the corners of her mouth. 'For instance, I bet you've been dying to give me a rundown on what I missed today.'

Jean flipped open the shorthand pad she'd been carrying and grinned. 'Now that you mention it . . . let's see. Warren Thomas wants to know if we've heard from the rest of the family.'

'And have we?'

'Nope. No proxies in today's post, either.'

'Well, there are still a couple of days left before the big showdown. Suppose you start phoning them tomorrow, Jean. Luke and I worked out a rough of what we want to tell them; I'll tape it later and drop it off at your room. Okay, what else?'

'Emily spoke to the vice-president from Evian, she's made arrangements to go and see the château they keep dangling in front of you tomorrow. I didn't think you'd want her on the loose there alone, so I said you'd want to make the grand tour, too.'

Caitlin sighed, pausing in front of the mirror and brushing out her hair. 'Well, it ought to be different from inspecting laboratories. Anything else before I take a quick shower?'

'That's about it. Unless you want to hear about the Marquis's latest phone call?'

'Just make a note for me to return his call. Maybe I'll even ask him over for a drink before we go home. He's a nice man, and I've been negligent, haven't I?' Caitlin caught a reflection of Jean's face in the mirror and she started to laugh. 'All right, all right. I've been darned near rude. Do me a favour and phone him for me. Tell him I've been busy and invite him here the day after tomorrow, say at six or so, for a cocktail.'

Jean smiled and scribbled a note on her pad. 'Well, that's about it. Will you need me tonight, or is that a foolish question?'

'I'll be out this evening,' Caitlin said, ignoring Jean's knowing smile. 'What time are we scheduled to leave for the château tomorrow?'

'A car's picking you up at nine—if you're sure that isn't too early.'

'Luke and I are going out to dinner,' Caitlin said quickly, a faint blush spreading over her cheeks. 'It won't be a late night.'

'Of course not,' Jean said mildly. 'Well, have fun.'

As soon as her secretary had left, Caitlin hurried into the bathroom. Lying back in a tub of warm water, the perfume from her bath oil surrounding her like a fragrant cloud, Caitlin closed her eyes and thought about Luke. For weeks after learning of his death, she'd dreamed about him. It was never the same dream, but the end of it never changed. His strong arms would close around her and his whispered words would brush against her ear.

'I'll come back to you, Cat,' his voice would promise.

And, always, she'd wake in the night with tears streaming down her face. At the time, the dream had been both a welcome release after the terrible emptiness of her waking hours and a cruel reminder of his death. She'd never allowed herself to believe in it, not after his watch and ring had been sent home, not after a stiff, formal letter had arrived telling them that his ashes had been interred in the tiny republic in which his death—an unfortunate accident, the letter called it—had occurred. Now with the memory of his kisses only hours old, Caitlin saw the dream as a premonition, one she wished she'd permitted herself to accept.

She stepped from the bath and wrapped herself in a fluffy bath towel. Luke would have to hear the whole, ugly story soon, she told herself, even though it would hurt him. A feeling of quiet despair stole over her as she slipped into her clothing. It was almost as if he refused to deal with the present, as if he loved a memory, a Caitlin who no longer existed. How could he care for her, she wondered uneasily, believing what he did?

'One step at a time, Caitlin Thomas,' she murmured aloud, brushing her hair until it gleamed with a dark lustre. A prayer, long forgotten since childhood, sprang into her mind.

'Grant me the serenity to accept the things I cannot change,' she whispered, 'courage to change the things I can, and wisdom to know the difference.'

Caitlin straightened her shoulders and glanced into the mirror. 'Wisdom to know the difference,' she repeated firmly, staring at her own reflection. Then she turned off the lights and locked the door to her suite behind her.

Downstairs, in the glittering lobby of the great hotel, Luke was waiting for her. The realisation sent a tremor of anticipation rocketing through her.

CHAPTER NINE

THE soft glow of candlelight lit Caitlin's hair with dark glints of red and gold. The trembling flame danced upwards into the dark, oak-beamed room, casting its flickering shadow across her face, turning her eyes into mysterious pools of jewelled light. The old, bare brick walls gave the small cellar café a sweet, intimate warmth. On a tiny stage a few tables from them, a dark-haired woman sang plaintively of love won and lost, her quiet, husky voice reminiscent of dry leaves drifting through a dark forest. The song rose to an anguished cry and the singer bent her head as the spotlight highlighting her delicate face winked to blackness. There was a second's silence, and then the crowd burst into applause, as the spotlight came on again and the woman smiled and bowed.

Caitlin leaned closer to Luke and placed her hand over his. 'I didn't think places like this really existed.'

Luke smiled and clasped her hand tightly in his. 'I'm glad you like it here, Cat. It is nice, isn't it?'

'It's wonderful,' she sighed. 'These tiny tables, that little man playing the accordion, the candlelight—it's all perfect. How did you find it?'

'Just luck,' he said a bit smugly, and she giggled.

'The same luck that led you to that wonderful old place where we had lunch, and that inn where we had dinner? Come on, tell me the truth.'

'Okay,' he said with a grin. 'I'll confess. I'd planned on taking you to all those places years ago, when we talked about going to Paris.'

'And you remembered?' She sighed and leaned her head against his shoulder. 'I'm so glad.'

His hand gripped hers tightly for a second and then he let go and picked up his brandy glass. In the glow of the candlelight, his face seemed filled with a tired wisdom. She'd hoped that tonight he might want to talk about the past four years, but when she'd broached the topic, he'd cut her off with a shake of the head. There was nothing to discuss, he'd said. He knew all about the need to survive: he had done what he had to do in order to get through the past few years, and so had she. He had no questions he wanted answered, he'd insisted, and she hadn't pressed him any further. She gazed at him over the rim of her brandy glass. Of course he had no questions to ask her, she thought. He'd already answered them all himself, crafting his answers in ways he could come to terms with and accept.

And she would let him do just that, at least temporarily, she thought defiantly. She would protect him until time could begin to heal the wounds she couldn't see, wounds that went far deeper than the scar visible on his cheek. When they got home, she'd take him to Big Sur, surprise him with the little cabin she'd built on the side of the cliff they'd both loved. There, the lonely stretches of white sand and the thundering waves pounding the rocks below would work their cleansing wonder on him. Only then, when he was ready to listen and understand, would she tell him everything. For now, it was enough that he still loved her.

'A penny for your thoughts,' Luke said softly. 'Or are you disappointed in the new, pragmatic man I've become?'

'You could never disappoint me,' Caitlin said quickly. 'I was just sitting here and thinking how different we are from the two people who parted from each other in California four years ago, and yet how much we're still the same.'

'Let's see how much the same we really are,' he said, smiling at her. 'Shall we see if we still remember how to dance together?'

They moved on to the tiny dance floor, and she settled into Luke's arms with a contented sigh. She felt the touch of his hand in the small of her back, the roughness of his tweed jacket under her cheek. His mouth was pressed against her hair, and her body followed his as if they had danced together only the day before. The accordion was playing softly, some sad, unknown melody that sounded as melancholy as she felt and she closed her eyes, surprised at the sudden rush of tears that dampened her eyelashes. The music changed, became a sweetly sorrowful rendition of a song they'd both loved, and she heard Luke whisper the words, 'I believe in yesterdays,' and she knew he had recognised it, too, and remembered. Her arms tightened around his neck and she forgot everything but the wonder of being held and cherished by the man she loved.

'I want to be alone with you, Cat,' he whispered huskily, and she turned her head so that her face was buried against his neck.

'Yes,' she murmured, unashamed of her need to hold him and be with him. 'I want that, too.'

He kept his arm around her as they wound their way back to their table. She smiled up at him as he signalled for their bill.

'Can we walk for a while?' she asked as they left. 'It's such a lovely night.'

'We can do anything you like, Cat,' he murmured, his arm tightening around her. 'Just so long as we do it together.'

She leaned her head against his shoulder and they walked down the winding street in companionable silence, two people locked together in a web of contentment and happiness.

'Do you want to stop for coffee?' Luke asked her as the brightly painted tables and umbrellas of a café came into view.

She shook her head, about to tell him that she only wanted to be alone with him, when suddenly he ordered her to stand still. Before she could answer, he darted into the midst of the tables. In less than a minute, he was back, a shy smile on his face, a nosegay of poppies clutched in his hand.

'For you,' he said solemnly, and Caitlin smiled over his shoulder at the wizened old woman who was selling flowers from table to table.

'Thank you,' she murmured, burying her face in the poppies. 'They're beautiful.'

'That's the only thing missing from my list, Cat. The list of places we were going to visit together. That field of poppies we talked about—you know what I mean.'

Her cheeks turned the same crimson blaze as the flowers and she nodded her head.

'We'll find it,' she said. 'I know we will.'

She snuggled back into the curve of his arm, thinking she'd never fit any place as well as this one, and they walked on, past the shadowed buildings, occasionally stepping into a tiny courtyard and stealing a hasty glance at the banked flowers and moonlight-spangled trees. Finally, at the foot of the Rue des Abbesses, Caitlin stopped and looked back at the steep hill behind them.

'I'm glad we walked down from Montmartre and not up,' she sighed.

'You're tired,' he said quickly. 'I'm sorry, Cat. I should have thought . . .'

'I'm not a bit tired,' she insisted, and then she chuckled softly. 'But my feet are. No, not a taxi,' she added quickly as he started to hail one that was cruising by. 'You said we could do anything I wanted, didn't you? Well, what I'd really like to do is take the Metro back to the hotel.'

'Are you worried about spending all my money?' he teased.

Caitlin grinned. 'Nothing so kind-hearted,' she said. 'I just love to pass through all those stations and see all those exotic-sounding names on the platforms.'

He started to laugh. 'Who can resist a girl who thinks the Metro is exotic? But we'll have to hurry, Cat, if we want to catch a train before they stop running for the night.' He grabbed her hand and started pulling her along with him towards the underground entrance. 'Come on, slowpoke. You always swore that someday you'd be able to run as fast as I can.'

'That was on packed sand at Big Sur,' she gasped, trying to keep up with him. 'Wait a second . . .' She reached down and snatched off her sandals. 'And I wasn't wearing these silly things. Okay, tough guy,' she challenged. 'Do your best!'

Laughing like children on a holiday, they sped towards the Metro station and raced down the stairs. Luke fumbled in his pockets for tickets. 'I know they're here somewhere,' he insisted while Caitlin made faces at him. 'Aha!' he said triumphantly, pulling two from his jacket pocket, and then they were through the turnstiles, running for the platform, charging into the train just before it pulled out of the station. A sedately dressed, white-haired gentleman looked up in surprise from his newspaper, and Caitlin and Luke fought to control their ragged breathing and grins, but then the dapper stranger, with absolutely no change of expression, closed one eye in a deliberate wink and they collapsed against each other in laughter.

'Okay, wise guy,' Caitlin said after she'd caught her breath, 'now you owe me a new pair of stockings.'

'It was worth it,' Luke grinned. 'Your time's improved. Not Olympic class, but . . .' He laughed when she scowled, and then he pulled her against him. 'Anyway, your form is still terrific,' he whispered.

'Luke!' she murmured, trying to sound outraged, but she smiled in contentment.

The lobby of the hotel was quiet and almost deserted. Luke waited while Caitlin got her room key and they went up in the lift in silence. At the door to her suite, Caitlin hoped her voice sounded more relaxed than she felt as a sudden shy nervousness overtook her.

'Come in for a while,' he said, unlocking the door. 'I'll phone down for something, if you like. Do you want brandy or cognac? Wine, maybe, or coffee . . .' Her words trailed off into a whisper and she turned to face Luke, her features pale in the faint light coming into the sitting room from the window.

'I don't want anything to drink,' Luke said quietly, shutting the door behind him.

'Are you hungry?' she asked, fighting against the nervous torrent of words that threatened to pour from her dry throat and lips.

'Not for food,' he murmured, and her heart began to race wildly. 'Don't turn on the light, Cat,' he said, reaching for her hand as she raised it towards the switch. 'Just come here . . . yes, like that.'

'Luke,' she whispered, as his arms went around her and she lifted her face to his, 'you haven't said anything about my ring. I . . . I hoped you'd notice that I took it off. I did it just before I left here tonight.'

'I noticed,' he said huskily, his hands moving slowly

along her back, his lips moving against her cheek. 'I notice everything about you, Cat. I always have. Like the little curl of hair that won't stay put, right here,' he whispered, his mouth against her forehead. 'And your lashes—the way they curl,' he said, kissing her closed eyelids. 'And I always loved this tiny bump here—it makes you more perfect, somehow,' he murmured, his mouth touching the bridge of her nose. 'But most of all, most of all, I've always loved your lips . . .' His words were lost against her mouth as he kissed her.

Caitlin sighed and leaned her body into his. Her hands moved up his arms, across his shoulders, until finally they cradled the back of his head, her fingers stroking the thick, dark hair, drifting down to touch his neck, then moving back to tighten against the back of his head, wanting somehow to mould herself to him, become part of his body and his mouth and his arms. Her lips slowly parted under the heated pressure of his, and the long-remembered, never-forgotten taste and scent of him filled her with longing and a feeling bordering almost on sorrow.

'Cat,' he whispered, the sound fierce, as if it were torn from the very depths of his soul, and she leaned back in his arms as his lips moved to her throat, searing her skin with their fevered touch. She reached under his jacket, her hands moving slowly along his chest, touching the hard, knotted muscle, impatient for the feel of his skin, and his hands mirrored hers, drawing her coat from her shoulders, coming back to move slowly to her waist, to her back, and then, finally, to her breasts. Caitlin sighed, covering his hands with hers, knowing he could feel the frantic beat of her heart beneath his fingers, feeling the trembling begin within her as his hands moved to the back of her dress and his fingers found the long zipper at her neck.

'It's been so long since I touched you, Cat,' he murmured, the sound of his voice thick and filled with need. 'It's been an eternity since I kissed you. All the nights without you, the days . . .' His mouth returned to hers, but his kiss was different now, urgent, demanding, and she willingly gave herself up to it, lost in the feelings so long denied her. She could never remember wanting him quite like this, never remember being this ready to slip past the invisible boundaries they'd always observed, and she knew it was more than need, more than desire. This moment, this act, would erase all the pain, all the doubts of the past. She sighed as the silk dress slipped down her shoulders and his hands touched her bare skin, stroking her gently, the slightly roughened feel of his fingers everything she remembered, more than she remembered.

The moonlight was streaming through the window, touching them both with pale, white fingers. Through half-opened eyes, she watched his face as he looked at her, as his hands caressed her, flushing her body with warm anticipation. Slowly, she raised her hand to stroke his cheek. In the soft wash of light, the pallid strip of skin on her finger where she had worn Justin's wedding-ring shone eerily. She shut her eyes tightly, trying to eradicate the spectre that suddenly seemed to have moved like a chill aura into the quiet room. Luke's mouth was on her throat, his kisses hot and urgent against the hollow in her shoulder, his lips moving towards the creamy swell of her breast. Without warning, the words he'd uttered earlier that evening rose like ice-tipped needles to pierce her consciousness. 'There aren't any simple definitions of good and evil any more,' he'd said. Had he created a past in which Justin was a martyr and she a pragmatic survivor? She shivered as the chill spectre seemed to move nearer.

'Caitlin,' Luke whispered, his breath warm against her ear, 'what's wrong? What is it?'

'I ... it's nothing,' she said rapidly, burying her face against his chest.

'Something's the matter,' he insisted, tilting her face up to his. 'Please, Cat, tell me what it is.'

'It's nothing,' she repeated. 'Really.'

He grasped her by the shoulders and held her away from him. 'Don't lie to me, Cat,' he said quietly. 'A minute ago, you wanted me as much as I wanted you. Now, everything's changed. What's happened?'

She shook her head and tears welled in her eyes. 'Just drop it,' she murmured brokenly. 'Please, Luke, for my sake.'

His voice became flat and cold. 'It's Justin, isn't it? You were in my arms and you started thinking about him.'

'No, no ... yes, it was Justin, but it wasn't the way you think,' she cried. 'It's just that everything is happening so quickly, changing so fast ...' She bit back the urge to tell him a truth he could not bear.

He stared at her with the same, unchanging expression on his face, and then he reached out and smoothed the tousled hair back from her face.

'Okay,' he said softly, 'okay, love, I understand. There's no rush, Cat. We have all the time in the world. Why not take it?'

She forced herself to return his smile as he bent his head and gently kissed her lips.

'Sleep well, Cat,' he murmured. 'And dream of me.'

She watched him as he walked away from her. At the last minute, as his hand touched the door knob, she moved towards him unsteadily

'Luke? Will I see you in the morning?'

'Why even ask me such a question?' he asked quietly, turning to face her. 'Of course you will. I want to be with you; you know that. You know how I feel about you, Cat.'

She nodded her head and managed to smile. 'Good night,' she whispered as the door closed softly behind him.

Caitlin caught her lower lip between her teeth and bowed her head against the cool, hard wall next to the door.

'That's just the trouble,' she murmured unevenly, her words seeming to fill the darkened room. 'How do you feel about me, Luke?'

CHAPTER TEN

THE late afternoon sun beat down on the group gathered on the terrace of Château Evian. Emily Thomas sighed happily as she licked the last bit of *crême fraiche* from her teaspoon.

'Hasn't this been the most marvellous day, Warren? This castle is superb.'

Warren nodded as he finished the last of the wine in his crystal glass. 'Indeed it is, Mother. And the food— you say all these things were produced on the estate, monsieur?' he asked, turning to the manager of the Evian property.

The small, dapper man smiled proudly 'But of course, monsieur. The vegetables, the cheeses, the wine, the fruit—even the duck was ours. I know Monsieur le Comte will be delighted to hear of your pleasure. And you, Madame Thomas?' he asked, smiling at Caitlin. 'You have been silent for some time. You have, perhaps, questions you wish to ask me?'

Caitlin shook her head and Luke's hand tightened on hers under the table. 'No, *merci, monsieur*. I am ... I am quite satisfied with what I've seen.'

Unseen by the others, her fingers returned the comforting pressure of Luke's. She glanced at him and smiled shyly, still caught up in the secret they shared.

They had reached the château late in the morning, coming upon it suddenly as their limousine rounded a bend in the narrow road they'd been following for more than an hour since leaving the autoroute. Château Evian was like something out of a fairy tale, a gleaming white confection of stone walls, towers and turrets set against the dark, embracing arms of an ancient forest. Its interior was magnificent. Vaulted ceilings and Gothic arches soared overhead. Sunlight streamed through old, leaded-glass windows, illuminating the delicately hued Flemish tapestries that hung on the walls. Emily oohed and aahed as Monsieur Graubert, the manager, took them from room to room, occasionally uttering embarrassing squeals of approval as he pointed out beds once slept in by long-dead kings and queens of France, but it was not until they'd stepped out on to one of the château's parapets that Caitlin's breath caught in her throat.

'Luke...' Her whispered word had been unnecessary, for the sudden pressure of his arm around her waist told her that he'd already seen the garden below filled with blood-red poppies swaying in the wind.

'This is our place, Cat,' he'd whispered huskily. 'I knew we'd find it.'

Most of what Monsieur Graubert had said since then had been lost on her. It was as if the storybook setting and crimson blossoms had combined to wipe away everything except her awareness of the man at her side. 'Do you not think that would be a fine plan, Madame Thomas?'

'What?' Caitlin stammered. Clearly, the manager was waiting for her to answer a question he'd posed, but she had no idea what it was. 'I'm sorry,' he said quickly. 'I ... I was thinking about the château, and I didn't hear what you said.'

'He said,' Emily repeated frostily, 'that they would be honoured if we would spend the night.' Her expesssion softened and she pursed her lips. 'I could have the room that Catherine de Medici slept in.'

Caitlin looked at Luke in confusion. 'I ... I don't think so,' she said hesitantly. 'We have to get back to Paris.'

His hand tightened on hers under the table. 'I think it might be a good idea, Cat. We have some things to attend to, and this is the perfect place for it.'

His words were so polite, so businesslike, she thought, but the message in his eyes was meant for her alone. She thought of the poppies and caught her lip between her teeth.

'I really think we ought to stay,' he said again, and she caught a gleam of mischief in his narrowed eyes. 'So long as Aunt Emily isn't nervous about it.'

'Nervous?' The old woman sniffed. 'What on earth is there to be nervous about, Luke?' She nodded at the manager and smiled haughtily. 'Monsieur Graubert says the château has all modern conveniences.'

Luke nodded thoughtfully. 'Oh, I'm sure it has. I just thought you might be put off by ... well, never mind, Aunt Em. It's not worth mentioning.'

Caitlin glanced at him and frowned. What was he up to, she wondered. There was laughter glinting in his eyes, and a purposeful set to his jaw.

'What's not worth mentioning?' Warren demanded.

Luke shrugged and pressed Caitlin's hand again. 'It's just that I know how you feel about rodents,' he said carefully, his eyes on Emily's face. 'Mice, rats, that sort of thing. They can't be helped in an old stone structure like this one, can they, Monsieur Graubert?'

The manager's smile wavered slightly. 'We have a slight problem, monsieur,' he admitted after a short silence. 'But it is kept under control.'

'I'm sure it is,' Luke said pleasantly. 'Using ecological means, I hope. Well, after all, there must be owls and hawks in the forest.' He glanced at Caitlin and she tried not to laugh. 'And I assume there are bats in those towers. They keep the rodents in check, don't they?'

The man glanced from Emily's white face to Caitlin's calmly interested one. 'Uh, indeed they do,' he said finally, eager to please. 'We, too, believe in ecological balance.'

'We're so glad to hear that,' Caitlin said, catching on to the spirit of the game. 'And I'm glad to hear that there are still wild creatures living in the forest, monsieur?'

'Oh, there are many, madame,' the manager said happily. 'Foxes, of course, even badger and wild boar. Why, just last week we killed a large male in the garden, not ten feet from this terrace . . .'

There was a clatter as Emily pushed back from the table and sprang to her feet. 'Warren,' she said in a quavering voice, 'I'm afraid we have to leave. My appointment at Dior,' she added hastily when her son frowned blankly. 'Remember? Tomorrow morning at ten?'

'That's too bad, Aunt Em,' Luke murmured, getting to his feet. 'Perhaps Caitlin and I should stay and look the place over a bit more.'

Emily nodded in a distracted fashion and took Warren's arm. 'Yes, of course. We'll send the car back for you in the morning.'

Caitlin pushed back her chair and stood beside Luke as the manager escorted Emily and Warren from the terrace. Luke grinned and put his arm around her waist.

'So much for getting rid of the dragon lady,' he said softly. 'You do want to stay the night, don't you, Cat?'

He bent and brushed his lips against her ear, and his kiss sent a thousand messages to her. She moistened her lips and spoke in a hushed whisper.

'I don't know,' she said hesitantly. 'I don't even have a toothbrush with me . . .'

He smiled and ran his hand along the curve of her jaw. 'I suspect Monsieur Graubert is equipped for such major emergencies, Cat.'

'Luke...'

'I want to be alone with you, Cat,' he said huskily. 'I want to kiss you, be close to you—find the world that was ours four years ago.'

She buried her face against his chest. 'Luke, I have so much to tell you...'

His lips silenced hers in a tender kiss. 'You just told me all I need to know, Cat. When I saw the poppies, I knew this place was meant for us. Please, Cat—give us this night.'

She could see the love and need in his face, and she knew it mirrored her own. With a tremulous smile, she agreed.

Their rooms were handsome adjoining chambers just off the sweeping, circular staircase on the second floor. Hers had once housed the king's mistress, M. Graubert assured them, and Caitlin had no reason to doubt his words once she saw the Aubusson tapestries on the walls and the massive, red-silk covered bed, its canopy emblazoned with the royal crest. As soon as the door had closed behind her, she whirled about in a delighted circle, her feet dancing lightly over the painted tile floor. There was a portrait of a woman over the fireplace, and she smiled as she glanced at it, wishing she had a gown like the one in the painting to wear for the evening. Surely such regal surroundings deserved the proper costume. She smoothed down the skirt of her grey wool dress and smiled. It would have to do, she thought, with a shrug. Not fit for a king's mistress, perhaps, but...

There was a knock at the adjoining door and her heartbeat quickened as the door swung open. Luke stepped into the room and grinned at her.

'Well, it's not the George V,' he said casually, 'but I guess it'll do.'

'Isn't it wonderful?' she laughed, moving towards him. 'I just wish I didn't feel so guilty for taking time away from work.'

He put his arms around her and drew her head against his chest. 'Work isn't everything, Cat. You have to get the most you can out of each day. That's something these past four years taught me.'

'You mean you won't have to be dragged out of your lab any more?' she teased, tilting her head back and looking up at him. 'That will be a change.'

'It's going to be hard to keep me in the lab at all when I know you're working just down the hall from me.'

'You mean . . . you want me to stay at Thomas's?' she asked slowly.

Luke laughed and kissed the tip of her nose. 'Of course I want you to stay, silly. Would I want to get rid of the best executive director we ever had?'

'But you're back now, and I thought . . .'

'You thought wrong. Besides, I want you near me, Cat. I feel as if I'm just re-entering the world, coming back to life. I couldn't do that without you.'

A swell of contentment washed over her and she nestled into his arms. 'That's nice to hear,' she whispered happily.

'You have told Clarke you're not taking that job, haven't you?'

'Clarke?' Caitlin closed her eyes and took a deep breath. 'Luke, about that job . . .'

'I know it's tough to pass up, Cat.'

'No, it's not that. You see, they made their offer a couple of months ago, and . . .'

'Caitlin, are you telling me you want to take that job?'

'No, of course not,' she said quickly. 'I've already told them that.'

She felt the tension flow out of his body and his arms tightened around her. 'Then you did contact them. I bet they can't believe they lost out to Thomas twice in a row.'

'Luke, please let me tell you about Clarke...'

He tilted her face up to his and her breath quickened as she saw the dark intensity in his eyes.

'No more business talk' he murmured softly. 'Not tonight, Cat. Tonight is just for us.'

The need to tell him that she had lied to him about Clarke when it seemed the only way to gain his support in the fight against Emily faded as his mouth met hers. She would tell him everything when he was stronger. Then, there would be all the time in the world, she thought with a sudden happiness. He loved her, and that was all that mattered. Her thoughts blurred into a kaleidoscope of colours as she gave herself up to his embrace.

'Luke,' she whispered as his lips moved softly along her neck, 'Monsieur Graubert...'

'He isn't going to bother us, darling,' he said huskily, kissing the hollow of her throat, her pulse beating wildly under the touch of his mouth. 'He sent his apologies, and said he had to leave for a few hours. We're to ring when we want dinner.' His arms tightened around her and she could feel the hardness of his body pressing demandingly against hers. 'But we don't want dinner, Cat, do we?'

She would not let Justin's ghost separate them tonight. With a sigh of joy, she wrapped her arms around his neck and pressed her lips against his neck, and her whispered response made him shudder.

'No,' she murmured fiercely, 'no... All I want is you, Luke. You, you, you...'

He lifted her into his arms and covered her mouth with his, and the searing flame that was his kiss made her gasp. Quickly, he crossed the room and laid her gently on the great, silk-covered bed, and as he stretched out beside her, her fingers fumbled at the buttons on his shirt, until finally she felt the heat of his skin and the steady beat of his heart under her hands. His mouth was the centre of her universe and her lips clung to it with desperate abandon.

He drew back and his eyes caressed her, the love and passion in them almost like the touch of his hands on her body.

'I love you, Caitlin,' he whispered. 'In this whole, crazy world, you're all that matters to me. I don't know how I could have ever forgotten that, even for a minute. I want to make you mine. But if this isn't the time, if you want to wait . . .'

Slowly, her eyes locked with his, she drew the shirt from his shoulders and ran her hands along the smooth skin she had never forgotten, stroking the hard muscles in his arms and back, glorying in the feel and the clean, masculine smell of his body.

'Make love to me, Luke,' she said unashamedly. 'Please, darling, make me yours.'

'Cat . . .' The word was a hoarse whisper, a declaration of love. His mouth covered hers again, sweet and demanding, telling her everything she had waited so long to hear. He drew back from her and she watched his face as he opened the buttons of her dress, her breath catching in her throat as he slid it off her shoulders.

'You're so beautiful, Cat,' he said thickly, 'so lovely . . .'

She sighed as he fumbled at the clasp of her bra, and then his hand cupped the soft curve of her breast and her sigh turned to a moan of pleasure as his mouth closed around the waiting swell of her flesh.

'Luke,' she whispered, 'Luke, listen . . .'

'Hush,' he growled. 'Don't say anything, Cat. Just let it happen, the way it should have years ago.'

'But I want to tell you . . . I want you to know . . .'

He raised his head. 'Do you want me to stop, Cat?'

'No,' she whispered quickly. 'It's not that.'

'Do you want me?' he asked in a hoarse whisper.

'You know I do,' she sighed. 'I always have.'

'Then stop talking, love. Stop thinking. Just feel, and want, and be mine.'

His mouth and hands silenced her, until she knew nothing but the wonder of this moment. Her fingers joined his, fumbling at her belt, hurrying the time when nothing would separate their heated bodies.

'Luke? Are you in there? Caitlin? Where in heaven's name are you?'

Caitlin's eyes flew open. 'Luke—it's Emily.'

'Don't be ridiculous,' he growled. 'She and Warren are halfway back to Paris by now.'

'Luke?' The voice was closer now, and suddenly there was a knock at the door in the next room.

Luke swore furiously and grabbed his shirt. 'I'll be right back,' he whispered. 'I'll get rid of her as fast as I can.'

Caitlin buttoned her dress with trembling fingers and followed him across the room, closing the door part way after him.

'What are you doing here, Aunt Em?' he demanded, and Caitlin shut her eyes as she pictured the look on his face.

'What am I doing here, indeed. These blasted foreign roads! The car broke down, can you imagine? The chauffeur left us on some god-forsaken road near the river. No lights, no houses, no petrol station . . .' Her voice rose in indignation. 'He told us to stay in the car and wait for him, but it got dark—pitch black, Luke—and so Warren and I decided to walk.'

'Yes, I can see that,' Luke said mildly. 'Is that manure on your shoes, Aunt Emily?'

Caitlin leaned against the door and clapped her hand over her mouth, forcing back a giggle.

'We had to tramp through potato fields,' the old woman said angrily. 'What on earth is the point of building a castle out in the middle of nowhere? These foreigners—their customs make no sense, Luke. None whatsoever.' Her voice dropped to an ominous whisper. 'You were right about rats, Luke. There was a strange squeaking sound in the hall downstairs...' Her voice rose again. 'I am not sleeping alone in this dreadful place, I can tell you that. Which is Caitlin's room? The housekeeper said it was large enough for two...'

'I don't think that's necessary, Aunt Em,' Luke said quickly, and Caitlin sighed as she smoothed down her dress and ran her fingers through her hair. She took a deep breath and flung open the door.

'Hello, Emily,' she said pleasantly, smiling apologetically as she walked past Luke. 'I'm sorry you've had such a bad time.'

Emily sniffed. 'I hope you don't mind sharing your room, Caitlin,' she said, stalking past her towards the open door of the adjoining room, 'but I shouldn't think you'd want to sleep alone in this dreadful place, either.'

Caitlin smiled sadly as she saw the anger and frustration in Luke's face. 'No,' she said softly, her eyes on his, 'I certainly didn't.'

When dawn touched its rosy fingers to the old glass window-panes, she was still lying awake next to the old woman, trying unsuccessfully to stop thinking of Luke lying alone in his bed in the next room.

CHAPTER ELEVEN

FLAT, heavy clouds the colour of old pewter hung over Paris the next afternoon, Caitlin turned from her sitting-room window and smiled at her secretary.

'All the books were right, Jean. This is the loveliest city in the world.'

Jean glanced out at the darkening sky and nodded. 'Sure, if you have gills. Haven't you noticed that it's been raining?'

Caitlin smiled. 'So what? Paris is still beautiful.'

Jean grinned. 'That must have been some trip you guys took yesterday. Emily came back convinced she never really wanted a château in the first place, and you came back looking smug as a cat that ate the cream.'

'It's just that I'm so happy—especially now that one of the proxy votes finally got here. And you're sure two of Luke's cousins are arriving tonight?'

'Yes, Caitlin,' Jean said patiently. 'There's nothing more to do until the meeting tomorrow. Oh, there is one thing—Clarke called again. They said there are some new developments that might change your mind about that job offer.'

'Nothing will change my mind,' Caitlin said impatiently, tossing aside the memo Jean had handed her. 'I've given them the same answer at least a dozen times. Send them a wire and tell them it's still no, will you?'

'Okay, then that does it.' Jean glanced at her watch. 'You have just enough time to change before you meet the Marquis in the bar for cocktails. You told me to call him, remember?' she said gently when Caitlin looked at her blankly. 'He'll be here at six.'

'Right. I almost forgot. I can just about make it; Luke will be here at seven to pick me up for dinner.' She hurried into the bedroom and began to lay out her clothes for the evening. 'I just hope he was able to get a call through to his lawyer,' she called over her shoulder. 'The time difference makes it hard to get through, and he had some things he wanted to sort out before we leave here tomorrow.' She paused and stared into her closet. 'I wonder if I should wear the white wool or the green?' she murmured. 'Luke always liked me in green . . .'

Jean grinned as she opened the door to the suite. 'I doubt if he'll notice,' she said. 'He's got that same dopey look on his face you have. I'll see you in the morning, Caitlin.'

'Good night, Jean.' Caitlin stuck her head around the bedroom door. 'Let me know if Luke's cousins arrive, okay?'

'I will, I will,' her secretary assured her. 'You just get ready to meet the Marquis. That poor man doesn't stand a chance and he doesn't even know it yet.'

As soon as the door had closed, Caitlin hurried into the shower, humming happily. It would be wonderful if Luke arrived early, she thought. Claude was one of Thomas's new clients; they'd have so much to talk about. How nice it would be to introduce them.

Shortly before six, she took a last, critical glance into the mirror and then made her way down to the hotel's elegant cocktail lounge.

She paused at the entrance to the handsome, already crowded room. The Marquis, elegantly attired as always, rose from his table and waved to her.

'Ah, my dear Caitlin,' he said in impeccable English, 'at last you've found time to see me.'

'Hello, Claude,' she said, smiling at him as he raised her hand to his lips. 'I'm terribly sorry I've been so hard to get hold of these past few days. But I've been so rushed, I haven't had a moment to spare. It's good to see you.'

'And I am delighted to see you, *ma chérie*. You look lovely, Caitlin. *La belle France* seems to agree with you.'

Caitlin slid into the seat opposite him and nodded her head. 'Oh yes, it does indeed. I wish I could stay in Paris for another week, at least.'

Claude smiled and signalled to the waiter. 'Two Kir on the rocks, *s'il vous plaît*. That is what you still prefer, is it not, Caitlin?'

'I'll always be indebted to you for introducing me to white wine and crème de cassis,' she laughed. 'Yes, please, a Kir would be fine.'

He leaned back and looked at her appraisingly. 'Well, are you going to tell me why you have that special look about you? It's more than Paris; I can tell that much without even asking. Has your business here gone well?'

She smiled and shrugged her shoulders. 'Who knows? It won't be concluded until tomorrow, and I'm afraid I'm not quite certain of the outcome yet.'

'I see,' he said, lifting one eyebrow. 'Then, I am puzzled. I have never seen you look so radiant, Caitlin. And I suspect it has nothing to do with me, unfortunately.'

She sipped at her drink and smiled again. 'There's someone here, someone I never thought I'd see again. And he means a great deal to me. Does that sound confusing?'

'No,' Claude sighed, shaking his head. He shrugged and raised his glass to her. '*Bonne chance*, Caitlin. I'm sorry I'm not the man who's brought that look to your eyes, but I'm very happy for you.'

'Thank you, Claude.' Impulsively, she reached across the table and took his hand in hers. 'I'm sure you'll like him. Actually, you'll deal with him quite often at Thomas from now on.' A smile lit her face as she looked across the room. 'He's here, Claude. You can meet him and then I'll explain. Luke,' she called, rising from her seat and waving, 'Luke, we're right here.' Caitlin sat down and looked at her companion questioningly. 'You don't mind if he joins us, do you? I didn't expect him this early, but at least you two will have a chance to meet.'

'I shall be delighted to meet this gentleman, Caitlin.' The Marquis squeezed her hand and grinned. 'It will be interesting to shake the hand of the man who can bring such a glow to your face.'

'Thank you, Claude.' She smiled and looked up as Luke reached their table.

'Hello, Cat. Don't bother getting up,' he said, turning to the Marquis. 'I wouldn't want to break up such a cosy little scene.'

Caitlin's eyes widened in surprise and she drew back her outstretched hand. 'I'm so glad to see you, Luke. I was just telling Claude about you.'

Luke smiled slightly as he sat down next to her. 'Really? Did you also tell him I wasn't due here for another half-hour, Cat?'

There was a brief, uneasy silence. The Marquis looked from Caitlin to Luke and cleared his throat. 'Caitlin tells me that you are soon to be the man I'll deal with at Thomas Pharmaceuticals.'

'And I'll just bet that broke your heart.'

Caitlin flinched and put her hand on Luke's arm. 'Luke,' she said quietly, 'this is Claude de Ville. He's been doing business with us for the past year. Claude, this is Luke Thomas.'

'Thomas?' the Marquis repeated. 'Does that mean that you and Caitlin are related?'

Luke's smile was unpleasant. 'Very much so. Caitlin is my sister-in-law. She was ... kind enough to manage things at Thomas for me these last few years. But all of that is about to change, isn't it, Cat?'

Claude looked at Caitlin and she forced a smile to her lips. 'Luke means I won't be trying to run things all by myself any more, Claude. He was always in charge of research and development, you see, back in the days when I was the office supervisor.'

'But surely you will not be back where you started, Caitlin,' Claude said, staring at her.

'Caitlin won't ever be back where she started, at least, not with me,' Luke said flatly. 'Anyway, why be so modest? Didn't you tell your friend you've got a much better job waiting for you?'

'Why, Caitlin, you never said a word about it ...'

She shook her head imperceptibly and Claude fell silent.

Luke smiled unpleasantly. 'You have to learn to be more open with your old friends, Cat. Or were you hoping for a counter-offer from Claude?'

Waves of bewildered confusion washed over her. Desperately, she stared at Luke, trying to make sense out of his sharp, cutting words, hoping for some clue that would explain his behaviour, but there was nothing to read in his flat stare except coldness and anger. With the greatest effort, she forced herself to smile at Claude in a way she hoped was reassuring.

'It's true, Clarke Labs offered me a job, but ...'

'The top spot, Cat. I'll bet it's at almost double the salary you're getting now, isn't it? Come on, don't be coy with us.' Luke leaned towards the Marquis and smiled. 'That's one of my sister-in-law's most priceless attributes, you know. She's so shy and unassuming.'

The Marquis's face darkened and Caitlin put a

trembling hand on his arm. 'Claude owns a pharmaceutical research company and we've been manufacturing his newest drug under licence,' she said quickly, trying to ease the tension and assemble her thoughts. 'We met when he came to California last year.'

Claude smiled politely and patted Caitlin's hand. 'Yes, that's right. I came to California to renegotiate our licensing agreement. I thought I'd be able to persuade Caitlin to agree to a higher royalty percentage for my firm in return for exclusive manufacturing rights for her.' He paused and Caitlin smiled nervously, her eyes on Luke's face. 'But I was wrong. Not only did we continue at the old percentage; somehow, I gave her the exclusive rights, anyway.'

'That's our Caitlin,' Luke said briskly, lighting a cigarette. He blew out a plume of smoke and smiled at her. 'You're a real miracle worker with men, aren't you, sister-in-law?'

Caitlin stared at him with a nervous smile frozen on her face. 'Claude,' she said at last, moving her chair back from the table, 'I know you'll forgive us, but we have to be going. Thank you for the drink...'

'There's no rush, Cat. I'd love to hear how you persuaded M de Ville to be satisfied with the old percentage and still give you exclusive rights to the drug.'

The Marquis frowned and toyed with his wine glass. 'I don't want to delay you, Caitlin,' he said, ignoring Luke completely. 'If you must leave...'

'I asked a question,' Luke said abruptly. 'Is it so difficult to give me a straight answer?'

Claude de Ville flushed and half rose from his seat. Quickly, Caitlin reached out and touched his arm. 'Claude, please,' she murmured, 'don't say anything. I'm sorry...'

'Come on, Claude,' Luke urged. 'You can tell me. I'm part of the family, remember?'

'What on earth is the matter with you, Luke? Caitlin hissed. 'Why are you acting like this?'

'Like what?' he asked innocently. 'I just want to know how you got the old boy to change his mind. Is it a secret?'

'It is no secret,' the Marquis said stiffly. 'Caitlin told me of the great need for the drug in developing countries. She explained how vital it was that Thomas manufacture it to keep the price low. It took her an entire evening to convince me, but finally I was in complete agreement with her.'

'Ah,' Luke said softly, nodding his head. 'Now I understand. Well, why not? After all, it took her just a little over a week to persuade my brother to marry her.'

Caitlin's face flushed with humiliation. 'Luke, please...'

'It's all right, Cat. You don't have to be shy about your accomplishments. You did get what you bargained for, didn't you, Claude?'

The other man shoved back from the table and got to his feet. 'That is quite enough,' he said softly. 'I have kept quiet, for Caitlin's sake, but now it must stop. You will apologise, monsieur, and at once.'

Luke pushed back his chair and stood up. 'Why not?' he said gruffly. 'I really have no right to involve you in this, have I? This is a family matter, after all.' He started to walk away and then turned back to Caitlin. 'I'll be waiting for you outside,' he said quietly. 'It's time to lay all our cards on the table.'

She watched in stunned silence as Luke strode through the crowded room and out of the door. Then, slowly, she stood up.

'Claude,' she whispered, 'I'm terribly sorry. I don't understand what's happened. Luke isn't like that.'

'Don't apologise, *ma chérie*. It is I who am sorry. For you, Caitlin. He has no right to treat you that way. If you will let me, I'll demand he apologise to you.'

She shook her head and managed a faint smile. 'No, no, I can handle it. It's just that, well, you see, Luke has been through a very bad time. I can't explain it now, but it's taken a toll on him. Otherwise, he'd never have behaved that way. Forgive me, Claude. I don't really know what to say to you.'

'You owe me no explanations, Caitlin. But that man owes one to you. To have a woman look at him the way you did, and then to treat her in such a fashion ... *Chérie*, are you certain you don't want me to deal with him?'

Caitlin patted his arm and assured him that she would be fine. 'I'll try and call you before I fly back to the States,' she said. 'Don't worry about me, Claude. Please.'

She hurried from the table, almost as embarrassed by the look of pity in Claude's eyes as she was hurt by Luke's behaviour. It was as though he'd gone back to where they'd been the first night he'd come to her suite, she thought, as if all his anger and bitterness had returned. She stepped through the doorway and gasped with surprise as Luke suddenly grasped her arm.

'What's the matter with you?' she whispered, tears filling her eyes as she stared at the enigmatic smile on his face.

He made no reply as he hurried her to the lift and they went to her floor in silence. She almost stumbled trying to keep up with him as they hurried down the corridor to her suite.

'Now,' she said, closing the door behind them and taking a deep breath, 'now tell me what this is all about. You embarrassed me terribly downstairs. And the Marquis ...'

Luke's eyebrows lifted and he whistled softly. 'The Marquis,' he repeated evenly, walking over to the couch and sinking down on it. 'I hope, for the Marquis' sake, that you and he were able to complete your ... negotiations without any interruption. You can't always be lucky enough to have Emily come knocking at the door, Caitlin—or have a man die, the way Justin did.'

The ugly words struck her with the force of a physical blow. 'That's enough,' she whispered. 'You'd better start explaining yourself, Luke.'

'Why did you marry Justin, Cat?' he demanded.

She stood up slowly and faced him. 'I've been trying to tell you that for days,' she said softly. 'Why do you suddenly want to hear the story now?'

'Just answer the question,' he said sharply. 'Did you love him?'

Caitlin shook her head. 'No, of course not.'

'When he married you, did Justin know you didn't love him?'

'Yes, he knew,' she said, her eyes on his.

Luke smiled coldly. 'He knew,' he repeated, and she nodded her head. 'But he wanted you anyway. I suppose he thought you'd change, that you'd grow to care for him. Is that what he said?'

'Yes,' she admitted, 'that's what he said. But I told him I wouldn't—that it would never happen.'

He turned away from her and walked to the window. 'Were you a good wife to him, Cat?'

So this is how it will end, she thought suddenly, looking at his stiffened back, his tensed shoulders. They had returned to square one, travelled in a circle back to the beginning, to the first night he'd come to her suite. The intervening days, the nights, the impassioned whispers and kisses, had only been detours, stop-gaps on the one-way road leading to this minute. The uphill struggle to regain their love had only been a path leading to a precipice. With a regisnation born of weary defeat and acceptance, she answered.

'I did what he wanted,' she said tonelessly. 'I ran his home, I went to parties with him, I accompanied him on business trips. Yes, I was a good wife, I suppose.'

'And was he a good husband?' He swung around and stared at her with cold intensity. 'Did he do his damnedest to make you happy?'

'Stop interrogating me as if this were a courtroom, Luke.'

'Come on, Cat,' he said bitterly. 'Let's deal in truth for a change. He was worried about you. You had no family, no one at all to turn to. And somehow, somehow, you twisted that sympathy he felt for you until he thought he had to take up where I'd left off. Isn't that right? He said he'd marry you, take care of you, and you promised you'd learn to love him. Isn't that the way it was?'

'Never!' she whispered.

'And you were planning to be such a good, devoted wife to him that you went to his lawyer's office two days after my "funeral"—two days, for God's sake— and sat there with him while his attorney drew a prenuptial agreement giving you voting rights to my stock.'

Everything that was happening began to fall into place like pieces of a puzzle. He had all the facts, but he had none of the reasons that explained them.

'That was the only way I'd agree to marry him.'

'Well,' he said slowly, 'at long last, the truth comes out.'

'And whose fault is that?' she asked, anger beginning to replace her fatalistic feeling of lethargy. 'You refused to listen to me all week.'

'You're right, Cat. For instance, the codicil to Justin's will. That was taken care of the very same day, wasn't it? You even dictated part of it when the wording didn't quite suit you, didn't you?'

'That's right. It was all part of our bargain.'

'Tell me, wasn't it enough that he'd agreed to give you his name and take care of you? Did you have some sort of premonition that you'd end up a widow in just six months?'

'Stop it,' Caitlin said sharply. 'You know that he died of an aneurism, and that no one knew about it until he collapsed.'

Luke leaned back against the wall and folded his arms across his chest.

'That's true,' he said coolly. 'I guess you were just lucky. Without that aneurism hiding in his artery like a time bomb, you might have been stuck with him for a lifetime.'

'I was prepared to stay with him forever,' she said, trying to remain calm. 'We had an agreement—which you still know nothing about,' she added quickly. 'You're just making assumptions . . .'

'What assumptions? That you conned my brother into giving you what you wanted? The Thomas name, the money, the corporation ... That's not an assumption, Cat. That's fact.' His eyes narrowed as they raked over her. 'And I can see what you gave him in return—although I'll never know why he'd have wanted it . . .'

'Luke . . .' Her voice held within it a sharp warning, but he ignored it.

'. . . because Lord knows he knew what you were.'

Fury mushroomed within her. For days, she had protected him from the truth, insulated him from reality, nurtured him with her love. She had been willing to ignore her own burning need to share with him the pain she had suffered these past years, driven by the conviction that his trauma had been far greater than hers. Love, compassion, time to heal—all these she had given freely, wanting nothing in return. With sudden clarity, she saw that she had also given up the one thing she must salvage. He would not—could not—strip away her honour, her self-respect.

'Prepare yourself for a shock,' she said angrily, her body trembling with rage. 'Justin wasn't quite the big brother you think he was. The truth of the matter is that he was always after me. Don't smirk, Luke,' she said quickly, her voice rising. 'For years, he skulked around in the shadows, touching me, whispering things . . .'

'Do you really expect me to believe this?'

'Whether you do or not is your choice. At least, you're going to hear the truth for once. I never told you about it because I didn't want to come between you. I knew you loved him, in spite of your differences, so I gritted my teeth and just tried to stay out of the way.'

'Except for that time you tried to talk me into selling out to Clarke.'

'You know why I wanted you to do that,' she said furiously. 'So you could be free of Justin . . .'

'Free to make a couple of million on the sale, and a nice little bundle for your five percent, too. Don't leave that out, Cat.'

'Damn you, Luke . . .'

He smiled coldly and shook his head. 'I think that's a fate reserved for you, my sweet sister-in-law.'

Caitlin slammed her hand against the wall and stalked across the room towards him. 'That's enough,' she stormed. 'You just shut up and listen to me for a change. God knows I've listened to you long enough. You're going to hear the truth, whether you're ready for it or not. All these days, I've kept quiet because you'd been through so much that I didn't have the heart to hurt you.' She paused and drew a deep breath. 'Well, now you're going to hear what I went through, what I lived through after they said you were dead, after I had nothing left to live for.'

'But you found something quickly enough, didn't you, Cat? You manage to make that sound like such a touching sentiment, but . . .'

'Keep quiet and listen to me, Luke,' she said hotly, her voice quivering with rage. 'You were dead, and I was empty inside. Justin made fun of that. He asked me if I was going to spend the rest of my life in mourning, and I said I was, in a way. That I'd keep your memory alive by working harder than ever, that if it were up to me, I'd set up a research fellowship in your name. And he . . . he just laughed at me. He said he was going to sell the company, get rid of it. I pleaded with him; I said you'd given your life for your beliefs, that all that was left of you in this world was the company you'd believed in. If it didn't exist any more, neither would you.' She paused for breath and her eyes searched his for some sign that he understood what she was saying. 'Don't you see? I didn't want Thomas swallowed up by a faceless giant, one that thought only in dollars and cents, the kind that wouldn't give a damn whether or not their drugs reached the people who really needed them. And Justin . . . Justin said he'd leave the company as it was, set up the fellowship, if I'd marry him.'

'Are you finished?' Luke asked in a cold, quiet voice. 'That's such a touching story, Cat, so romantic. It almost brings tears to my eyes.'

'It's the truth,' she raged, clenching her fists. 'And it's an ugly, terrible story. But you're going to hear the end of it, Luke.'

'By all means,' he said politely. 'I'm fascinated.'

'When I finally realised Justin was serious,' she said, forcing herself to keep her voice under control, 'I told him I'd marry him. I demanded that pre-nuptial agreement so I could hold him to his promises. And I told him he'd have to change his will so that Emily wouldn't get everything when he died, so that what I'd done, what I'd given myself to him for, wouldn't be lost. Now do you understand?'

Luke leaned forward and ground out his cigarette in the ashtray. When he lifted his head and looked at her, his eyes were cold and empty.

'Bravo,' he said softly. 'That was a magnificent performance. Outstanding. The only problem is, I don't buy any of it. You see, Cat, you overplayed your hand. I know all about survival; I told you that before. I knew you married Justin for what he could give you, and I was willing to accept that, to forget about it, because you did what you thought you had to do, to survive. I don't know why you went to the trouble of making up this entire scenario . . .' He paused only inches from her, his face twisted with pain and anger. 'How could you do it? You sold yourself to me so I'd influence Emily and the others, get them to vote against the merger because you wanted to bring Evian et Frères to Clarke, to your new employer, on a silver platter.'

Caitlin stared at him in disbelief. 'What are you talking about?' she whispered. 'I told Clarke I wasn't interested . . .'

'Don't lie to me, dammit,' he shouted. 'What happened, Cat? Was your price for selling Thomas too high? Or was it dependent on letting them get Evian first?' His hands shook as he pulled out a cigarette and lit it. 'I just spent the afternoon on the phone to San José, Cat. Jack—my attorney—spent the past few days tying loose ends together for me so it would be easier for me to pick up the pieces when I get back to California. One of the things he did was to contact Justin's lawyer. That's how he found out about your pretty little performance with the will and the marriage agreement. He thought I should know the legal status of Justin's property, you see.'

'The stock is yours, Luke. I told you I'd give it to you...'

'You told me lots of things,' he said quietly. 'How come you didn't tell me about Clarke?'

'I did,' she said quickly, backing away from him. 'They offered me a job, and I turned it down.'

'Stop it, Cat. The game is over. You ought to know by now that this business is one tight little community. Jack is friendly with some of the people on the board of directors at Clarke Labs. When I told him there'd be no legal problem recovering my stock or Justin's, that you'd agreed to return it to me, he was stunned. He said he couldn't imagine that Clarke would sit still for that.' Suddenly, Luke lunged forward and grasped her by the shoulders. 'How long have you known that Clarke made an offer to buy Evian, Cat? Was it your idea to keep us from merging with Evian so Clarke could get them at a bargain price, or was it Clarke's?'

'That's insane,' she whispered, the blood draining from her face. 'I don't know anything about it, Luke. I haven't even spoken to anybody from Clarke since we've been here...'

'What's the deal, Cat? Is it too much for Clarke to swallow Thomas and Evian together? Will it be easier for them to swallow up one company at a time?'

Caitlin winced as his fingers bit into her shoulders. 'Please, you must believe me. I had one meeting with Clarke. It wasn't even that; someone from their board called me and we had lunch together, weeks ago. He made the offer and I turned it down. Luke...'

'Is that why they've been calling you ever since you got to Paris? No, it's all over. It's finished. I told Jack to start proceedings against you so that I can recover my stock. And tomorrow, I'm going to persuade everybody to vote for the merger.'

'You'll lose everything Thomas stands for,' she whispered desperately.

'It's lost anyway,' he growled. 'You weren't going to give my stock back to me. This way, you'll go to your new employer with empty hands, Cat. They won't want anything to do with you. You've lost, Caitlin. You're finished.'

'I've lost?' she repeated dully, raising her eyes to stare into his. The weight of his accusations bore down upon her until she felt as if she could not draw breath into her lungs, and a final, blinding fury seized her. 'Damn you for a fool, Luke Thomas,' she exploded. 'You don't know what losing means, but you're going to learn! You'll never get your company back. Your stock is in my name, and Justin's is legally mine, Luke, just you remember that. I'll tie your claims up in court until hell freezes over.'

She stood her ground, watching as his face whitened with anger. An eternity seemed to pass until, finally, he shrugged his shoulders and a rueful smile twisted his mouth.

'Do what you want, Cat. I'll get back what's mine, no matter what tricks you pull. All the things you did, with Justin, with me, all that was for nothing.'

Tears of anger and despair streamed down her face and she turned away from him. 'You're like a stranger,' she whispered. 'I feel as if I never knew you at all.'

'That's supposed to be my line, isn't it?' he said

harshly. 'Just tell me one last thing. You knew you already had me in your pocket. Last night—was that all . . . all part of some master plan, or did you really feel something for me?'

Somewhere deep within her, her last shred of pride struggled to burst free. She squared her shoulders and lifted her chin. 'What do you think?' she asked, her eyes locked with his.

Time seemed to stand still around them. Then, Luke stepped back from her and shook his head.

'I guess that really was my line,' he murmured. 'I never knew you at all, Cat, did I?'

Caitlin shivered and turned away from what she saw in his eyes.

'No,' she said softly, 'no, I guess you never did.'

CHAPTER TWELVE

Two hours later, Jean Barrows stood in the doorway to Caitlin's bedroom, watching with ill-disguised dismay as her employer snatched her clothing from the dresser drawers and tossed it carelessly into the open suitcase on the bed.

'I can't believe you're doing this, Caitlin. And you weren't even going to tell me you were leaving, were you? If I hadn't called to tell you that Luke's cousins had arrived, you'd have just left without so much as a word.'

'I was going to stop by your room before I left, Jean. I just didn't want to waste any time.'

Caitlin brushed past her secretary and peered into the sitting room of the suite. 'Did I forget anything that you can see? No, I guess not. Hand me those slippers, will you?' she asked, going back into the bedroom. 'They're right under that chair ... If I forget anything, just bring it back with you when you fly home, okay?'

Jean's sigh of resignation seemed to fill the room. 'Sure, don't worry about it. But can't you at least wait until morning?'

'I'm leaving right now,' Caitlin said firmly as she scooped her make-up and toiletries into a leather carry-on bag. 'You did phone down for a taxi, didn't you?'

'Yes, I did just as you asked, Caitlin. Your flight leaves in just over an hour from Orly.' Jean reached into the suitcase and absentmindedly began neatly folding the clothing inside it. 'But you'll have to make your own arrangements once you get to New York. The airline couldn't confirm space on the connecting flight to San Francisco.'

'Will you please stop worrying about me? I'll be fine, really. I will, I promise,' she said, reaching down and hugging Jean. 'You just stay here and help Luke tomorrow.'

'Help him?' Jean sputtered. 'You have to be joking.'

'Jean . . .'

'All right, whatever you say,' she sighed, throwing up her hands in resignation. 'What do you want me to do?'

Caitlin sat down beside her and smiled. 'Nothing terribly difficult. Just two simple things, that's all. First, I want you to give him my blank proxy in the morning.'

'You're not joking,' her secretary said slowly, 'you've lost your mind. He's going to vote for the merger, Caitlin. You told me that yourself.'

'And I also told you that Thomas is Luke's company. He's entitled to do whatever he likes with it, now, isn't he?'

'I suppose so, but . . .'

'And then,' Caitlin said quickly, rummaging through a stack of papers piled on the bedside table, 'then, as soon as the meeting is over, give him this.' She handed Jean a long white envelope. 'It's a letter I've written to Luke. Well, actually, it's a statement. I'm turning over all the stock I inherited from Justin to him. Don't look at me that way, Jean. It's his, after all.'

'You don't really mean all of it, do you? His shares, maybe, but . . .'

'All of it,' Caitlin said firmly.

'Caitlin, for heaven's sake, you're entitled to Justin's portion. No court in the world would take those shares from you.'

'Probably not,' she agreed quietly.

'Well, then...'

'Look, Jean, if I took him to court, what would be the purpose of everything I did?' Caitlin shook her head emphatically. 'No, it's got to be this way. But you must remember, Jean, you're to give him this statement only after the meeting ends, no matter how the merger vote goes.'

Jean looked at her blankly. 'But why then, Caitlin? Let me give it to him first thing in the morning. Maybe he'll think twice about what happened.'

Caitlin shook her head and got to her feet. 'He doesn't trust me,' she said quietly. 'He'd think I was trying to trick him, to influence him for some ulterior motive. Besides,' she added, buttoning her coat, 'I know how Luke feels about Thomas Pharmaceuticals. Once the chips are down, I'm betting that he won't want to merge his company with an outfit like Evian, no matter how much he despises me.'

'Okay,' Jean said glumly. 'I'll do it your way. But you're putting an awful lot of faith in a man who's knifed you in the back.'

'I don't have ny choice, Jean.'

'If you say so, Caitlin. I just hope you know what you're doing.'

'I hope so, too. My track record for making the right moves isn't terrific, is it?' Caitlin placed the shoulder strap of the leather bag over her arm and reached down for the suitcase. 'Well,' she said finally, 'I guess that's everything...'

Jean rubbed her hand across her eyes and grabbed the handle of the suitcase. 'Where on earth is that porter?' she said gruffly, turning her back to Caitlin. 'Never mind; I'll help you down with this.'

The two women took the lift down to the lobby in silence. At the kerb, Jean handed Caitlin's suitcase to a burly taxi driver, and then she flung her arms around her employer.

'I'll see you in San José in a few days,' she muttered. 'You just take care of yourself.'

'I will,' Caitlin promised. 'You remember to give those things to Luke tomorrow, all right?'

'Sure,' her secretary said, sniffing loudly. 'You can count on me.'

Caitlin climbed into the waiting taxi and slammed the door. She looked back and waved as Jean's figure grew smaller and smaller, and then the brave smile she wore faded from her face. In the rain and darkness of the night, Paris seemed suddenly old and tired. The deserted streets looked like worn stage sets beneath the merciless clarity of the glaring street lights. Even the rain-drenched grey buildings seemed to be huddling together for comfort. Wearily, she laid her head back against the torn leather seat and closed her eyes.

What an absolute mess she'd made of things, she thought. If she had only laughed in Justin's face, ignored his terrible offer, none of this would have happened. Luke would have returned to her, still wanting her, still believing in her. And yet... He would have come back to the death of all his dreams, to a perversion of the very ideals he'd been willing to give his life for. That was why she'd made her bargain with the devil, she told herself, sitting up a little straighter. She had done it because Luke's life was over, and, in a way, hers had been over, as well.

'I'd do it again,' she murmured aloud, and the cab driver glanced into the rear view mirror and smiled.

'Pardon, madame?'

'Rien,' she said quickly. 'Nothing, monsieur, nothing at all.'

She kept her eyes closed for the rest of the trip, feigning sleep. When they arrived at the airport, she was surprised at how busy it was, even at such a late hour and she merged gratefully into the faceless throngs of people. Automatically, she picked up the ticket waiting for her and moved mechanically to the weigh-in counter. Someone directed her to the correct boarding gate and then, at last, a professionally cheerful flight attendant took her carry-on bag from her and motioned her to a seat in the almost deserted first-class cabin.

Caitlin settled back in her seat as the 747 began to taxi towards the runway. Within moments, they were racing against the jealous pull of the earth, and then the plane was climbing into the night sky, leaving the rain-swept stretches of the airport far below. Caitlin pressed her forehead against the cool glass of the window, watching as the clouds swallowed up the winking lights of the city, until finally she could see only the black, impenetrable night sky.

Luke was down there, far below her, she thought suddenly. Was he thinking of her even now while she was thinking of him? A sudden chill ran through her body. If he was, it was not quite the same, she knew. That look she'd seen on his face, the hatred in his eyes ... She could go on without him, as she had these past years, but to know that he despised her, that he believed her capable of such scheming, sordid cruelty ... She shuddered and wrapped herself in the blanket lying on the empty seat beside her. With careful deliberation, she moved her seat back and then closed her eyes.

At least she'd be home soon. But where was home? Surely it wasn't the big house in San José, the one she'd moved out of immediately following Justin's death? And it wasn't even the apartment she'd taken near Thomas Pharmaceuticals. There was nothing there that meant anything to her, nothing of her own. The only benefit of the tiny three rooms had been their proximity to the office. Not for anything would she want to face the empty silence of that apartment and the little patio from which you could see the rectangular brick shape of the Thomas laboratories.

She felt as lost and anguished as she had when the news of Luke's death had reached her. That day, she had fled to the bluff overlooking the sea at Big Sur, the one place that had been so special to them both. And her agonising decision over whether to marry Justin or not had been thought through there, after she'd scrambled down the bluff and walked for hours in the clean sand. The one extravagance she'd allowed herself after Justin's death had been that bluff. She had traced the name of its owner and then wheedled that acreage from him, paying the first sum he named without a second's hesitation. A local contractor had built a cabin on it for her, facing the endless expanse of the ocean, nestled snugly into the side of the cliff as it sloped down to the deserted beach below. The cabin had become a haven, a cave to retreat to whenever loneliness and depression had threatened to overwhelm her. No one knew of its existence; her only neighbours were the wheeling sea birds overhead, and an occasional sea otter diving for abalone just off shore. It was a rough cabin, not at all the kind of thing a home decorator would find pleasing. It was sparsely furnished, not winterised—but there was a fireplace on one wall, and she had bought herself a down sleeping bag at the little camping supply store just up the road in Monterey . . . Caitlin sat up straight in her seat and signalled for the flight attendant.

'I wonder if you could give me some information, if you have it. I know the flight connecting from New York to San Francisco is booked—I checked before we left Paris. What I was wondering was, what about one to Los Angeles? I want to get to Big Sur, and it really doesn't matter to me if I drive down there from San Francisco or up from L.A. I just want to get to Big Sur—get home—as fast as I possibly can.'

The flight attendant smiled. 'Well, Mrs Thomas, I can't guarantee it, of course, but there are almost always more flights to L.A. than to San Francisco. Matter of fact, I know there are at least two leaving within forty minutes of our arrival at Kennedy Airport. I'd almost bet you can get a seat.'

Caitlin sighed with relief. Perhaps in her tiny cabin overlooking the ocean, the wounds she'd suffered during the last terrible hours would begin to heal.

CHAPTER THIRTEEN

THE stretch of coastline called Big Sur in California lies alongside a narrow highway that twists and turns high above the Pacific Ocean. On one side of the winding road rise redwood trees, great brown and green sentinels guarding the land from the sea; on the other, ancient cliffs fall away to the white sand beaches and the foam-capped, blue-green water of the Pacific. Caitlin had driven over this highway more times than she could remember, always in awe of the primitive beauty surrounding her and the eternal struggle of land against the sea. The winding road became treacherous at the whim of the weather; rockslides and mudslides sometimes made sections of it impassable, but fog rolling inland from far across the vast ocean was the greatest danger of all.

Caitlin looked across the highway towards the water as she stepped out of the small, general store and frowned. The storm that had been predicted was moving in faster than expected; already, the ocean had darkened and a milky covering seemed to be settling over its depths. She shifted the grocery bag she held in her arms so she could reach into her pocket for her car keys. This was her second trip into Monterey in as many weeks; the small supply of canned goods she kept in the little cabin at Big Sur was dwindling and so were the contents of her wallet. She wouldn't be able to put off her return to San José much longer, she thought, as she drove out of the parking lot and headed south along the coast highway. She glanced down at the fuel gauge of her car; there was barely a quarter of a tank of petrol left in the little Datsun she'd rented the night she arrived in Los Angeles. Thank heavens for credit cards, she told herself. Still she needed her clothing, her own car, the money in her bank account . . . Soon, she sighed, she'd have to leave the security of the cabin on the bluff and go to San José.

The sun was a pale disc overhead, fighting against the encroaching fingers of a swift-moving, milky fog. She switched on her headlights and drove with careful concentration. The road was free of traffic, but the swirling mist had already begun to blur the fine line between it and the precipice beyond. Caitlin sighed with relief when the dirt tracks leading to the cabin finally came into view. Slowing the car, she pulled off the highway and followed the sharply pitched trail as it headed downward. Neither the car nor the cabin was visible from above unless you stood at the very edge of the bluff. An occasional hiker or stranded motorist ignored the discreet 'private property' sign posted at the start of the dirt track and wandered down to knock at the door but for the most part, once she reached the cabin, she left all contact with the world behind.

She parked the car and walked the last few yards through the hardy grasses and tiny wildflowers that held tenuously to the packed sand and rocks. The cabin was chilly and, as soon as she'd dumped her package on the wide-planked redwood table that stood in its centre, she went to the fireplace and lit the wood and kindling neatly piled inside. By the time she'd put away her few purchases, the flames were beginning to radiate a comforting warmth throughout the room.

The fog was at the windows now, curling its delicate tendrils around the cabin, obscuring the spectacular view of the ocean below the bluff. Caitlin lit a propane lamp to chase the shadows from the room and set a pot of coffee to perk on the fireplace grate. Far in the distance, she could hear the faint bleat of a ship's horn and once in a while the sound of a car engine broke the silence, but she knew from long experience that the sounds could have come from almost any direction; the thick fog seemed to play games with noise, toying with it like a cat with a ball of wool until it was impossible to tell where it had started.

She settled into a wooden rocking chair before the fireplace, her feet tucked up under her, and picked up an Agatha Christie paperback, the same one she'd been trying to finish for the last week. For several minutes, she held it closed in her lap and then she sighed, tossed it aside, and reached for the classified section of the past Sunday's newspaper. Dutifully, she re-read the advertisements she'd circled in the employment section, but finally she shrugged and put the paperback on the table.

It was useless, she admitted reluctantly. There were several ads for executives with degrees in business administration, but her field of expertise was a limited one. She knew all the details of the pharmaceutical industry and little about any other, but it would be impossible to get a job in her field with a California firm. Who knew what rumours Luke or his attorney might have spread about her by now? The only way to leave her past life behind and yet remain in her own field would be to move, perhaps to New York or Chicago, and start again. She closed her eyes and leaned her head back against the rocker, listening to the faint sound of the crackling fire against the backdrop of the building waves hitting the shore far below the cabin.

The past two weeks had put everything into perspective. For the first few days, she had done little except walk along the deserted beach and think about Luke. She felt as if her life had come apart once again, as if all the fabric of her existence had unravelled. Once, she'd stumbled on a young couple embracing in a quiet cove and, without warning, tears had filled her eyes. Even the plaintive cries of the seagulls that dipped and soared over the white sand had been enough to make her cry. But, gradually, as the days wore on and the sharp pain of their parting had begun to recede, it was replaced by a new determination to put aside her old life. Luke was alive, but their parting had achieved a finality that transcended even what she had felt that hot summer day when she'd sat with bowed head and listened to the minister eulogise his death. She had mourned Luke for four long years; the time had finally come to put an end to it.

She thought of the note she'd posted to Jean, assuring her that she was well, telling her that she'd be back to pick up her things sooner or later. She'd been careful to post it from Los Angeles without any return address, but eventually Jean would go through her things, turn up the deeds to this cabin, and find her. Better to show up in San José before that happened, Caitlin thought. But not today, not in this fog that had turned the cabin into a tiny island in a sea of white. And not tomorrow, either. Perhaps the day after that ... or the following week...

The sound of a car engine drifted down to her and she frowned. The fog, playing its tricks again. It must be; no driver would be so foolish as to attempt the narrow curves of the coast highway in this weather. She sat up straight, straining to hear, positive she'd picked up the faint sound of footsteps trudging through the gravel just outside the cabin. It was impossible to think someone was out there, trying to feel his way down the steep path, she thought, when suddenly there was a knock at the door.

Caitlin frowned in disbelief. There was, indeed, somebody out there, some fool who hadn't believed the road warnings. Whoever it was, he was damned lucky to have got this far. She got to her feet and stalked to the door. If the weather report was accurate, the fog was going to get worse and a storm would be moving in. She'd be stuck with a nervous, chattering stranger for hours.

'Yes, what is it?' she said irritably, wrenching open the door. 'Didn't you pay any attention to the fog warning before you . . .' The sharp words died in her throat as she gaped at the tall figure silhouetted in the mist. 'Luke?' she whispered. 'Luke?'

His face seemed a shadowed, mysterious series of planes and angles under the pulled down peak of a Greek fisherman's cap, but there was no mistaking the anger in his voice when he answered her.

'Exactly how long did you think you could get away with this game of hide and seek, Cat?'

She squared her shoulders and took a deep breath. 'I don't have the slightest idea of what you're talking about,' she said coldly. 'You're not welcome here, Luke. There's a sign up on the road that says this place is private property. Didn't you bother to read it?'

'I read it,' he said flatly, brushing past her as he entered the cabin. 'You'd better close that door, Cat, unless you want everything in here to get damp.'

She hesitated, shivering in a sudden gust of wind, and then she slammed the door shut and turned to face him.

'I have nothing more to say to you,' she said quietly, brushing her fog-dampened hair back from her face. 'I don't know why you came here, or how you found me, but I'd appreciate it if you left.'

'I came here to settle things, once and for all.'

'We did that in Paris,' Caitlin said quickly.

'I said I came to settle things,' he repeated evenly, 'and I'm not leaving until we do.' He looked around the small room and then back at her. 'So this is where you've been these past two weeks. Did you really think I wouldn't find out about it? You shouldn't leave land deeds tucked into the office safe, Cat.'

Caitlin bent and warmed her hands before the fireplace, her back to him. 'I bought this land with my own money, Luke, with dividends from my shares and money my father left me. And I built this cabin the same way. You have no rights to this place, none at all. I gave back everything that was yours.'

She straightened up as she heard his swift footsteps behind her, swinging around to face him just as he grasped hold of her arm.

'Why did you run out in the middle of the night in Paris?' he demanded angrily.

He had pulled off his cap and she could see his face clearly. There was a bright hardness in his eyes and a whiteness around his mouth that made her feel a sudden, apprehensive chill, but she forced herself to stand still and face him calmly.

'I didn't run out. We'd said all we needed to say to each other, and there was no reason for me to stay.'

'That's not true,' he growled. 'You'd just spent days telling me how important the future of Thomas Pharmaceuticals was to you. I thought at least you'd wait and find out what happened at the meeting the next day. Didn't you want to know whether or not the board accepted the Evian offer?'

Caitlin pulled free of his restraining hand and turned to the fireplace. 'Thomas is your business now, not mine,' she said steadily, filling a mug with coffee from the steaming pot. 'Anyway, you got what you wanted, didn't you? Emily must have been delighted.'

'Emily isn't talking to me. The merger vote failed.'

She closed her eyes at the flatness in his voice. 'I see,' she said slowly. 'I'm sorry if that's not what you wanted . . .'

'What I want are some straight answers,' he said quickly, 'but I can't seem to get any. Your secretary speaks only when spoken to, and then only in monosyllables.'

Caitlin spun around and stared at him. 'Wait a minute. The vote failed . . . Didn't Jean give you the things I left for you? The proxies and the stock transfer? I can't believe she forgot; she knew how important it was.'

He pulled a long, white envelope from the pocket of his faded denim jacket and tossed it on to the redwood table.

'She gave me the stuff, Cat. I've been carrying that around with me for the past two weeks.'

'Well, then,' she said slowly, staring at the envelope, 'I don't see . . . wasn't Emily satisfied with . . . with what I did?'

A smile lifted the corners of his mouth and he shrugged his shoulders. 'She was delighted that you missed the meeting. As for the stock,' he said, nodding at the envelope, 'it's none of her business.' His smile broadened into an open grin. 'There isn't going to be any merger because I persuaded most of my cousins to vote against it, and that's how I voted your shares, too. You were right about Evian all along. Let Clarke have them; I have the feeling they'll probably choke on them. I tried to tell you that after Jean gave me your proxies, but when I got to your suite, you were gone.'

She stared at him without comprehension, trying to make sense out of his words, wondering why he was looking at her so strangely.

'Did you hear what I said, Cat?'

She nodded her head and set her coffee mug down on the table. 'Yes, I heard you, Luke. I'm glad you decided against the merger. But I'm surprised you came to find me that morning. Weren't you afraid I'd jump for joy, tuck Evian into my pocket, and rush off to sign on with Clarke Labs? Or is that why you're so angry? Did you count on the pleasure of seeing me do that?'

He crossed the empty space between them in two long strides and took hold of her shoulders.

'Angry?' he asked roughly. 'Is that what you think I am? Crazy is closer to it, Cat. Crazy with worry, crazy from wondering where you'd gone, where you'd vanished to . . .'

'I can take care of myself,' she said stiffly.

'I don't think so, at least, not based on that move you tried to force on Jean,' he growled. 'Why did you tell her to give me that envelope after the meeting? Thank God she didn't listen to you. After she told me everything, after I realised you'd turned all the stock over to me, I knew everything you'd told me had been the truth.'

'The truth!' A sound that was neither a laugh nor a cry escaped from her throat and she shook her head in disbelief. 'What do you know about the truth, Luke Thomas? You ran away from the truth every minute we were together in Paris.' Her eyes met his and then she turned her head away. 'Look, this is pointless,' she added, trying to steady her voice. 'We've been all through this before. Thanks for telling me about the merger. I really appreciate it. If there's any legal difficulty about the stock transfer, have your laywer draw up the necessary papers and I'll come in and sign them. If you leave now, you can just about make it up the road before the fog . . .'

'Dammit, Caitlin.' He grasped her chin and forced her face back to his. 'Didn't you hear a word I said? I didn't come here to talk about the merger or the stock. Will you please stop being so damned polite?'

'What would you prefer?' she asked, trying to ignore the loud hammering of her heart. 'Would it be easier for you if I yelled, or got angry? Or maybe you'd like it better if I cried? Well, I'm not going to do any of those things, Luke. You have your company back. What more do you want?'

'I didn't come here to talk about the company. Haven't you figured that out by now?'

'Then why did you come here?' she whispered.

'If you'd keep quiet for five minutes, I'd tell you,' he said gruffly. 'I've spent two whole weeks planning this moment, trying to figure the best way to tell you how wrong I was...'

She wrenched free of his hands and backed away from him. 'It's a closed book, Luke. That's why I left you that letter. The stock, the company, it all belongs to you. We have nothing more to say to each other.'

He crossed the room towards her, his eyes flashing with anger. 'I don't want the damned stock,' he rasped. 'It's yours. You own it.'

'You mean I earned it, don't you?'

'Cat, please...'

'I'm not going to listen to you,' she said quickly. 'That's all I did while we were in Paris. I listened while you told me how hurt you were, how confused, how bitter. And then I listened while you told me exactly what you thought of me. Well, I'm tired of listening.'

'Cat, that last night in Paris...' He ran his hand through his hair and shook his head. 'I said I knew all about survival, what a person does just to go on living. I could handle that part of what you'd done—what I thought you'd done. But when I thought you'd lied to me about how you felt, used me just to tie up Evian so you could get that job ... I couldn't stand it, Cat. Don't you understand?'

'I understand everything,' she whispered, the tears she'd been fighting welling in her eyes. 'I was a fool, Luke, from the minute you first showed up in my hotel. You were too angry to listen to reason, so I made my first mistake. I let you think I wanted that job with Clarke just so I could get you to help me oppose the Evian merger. And then things only went from bad to worse. I tried to tell you the truth about Justin—God, how I tried—but you convinced me that the past didn't matter, that we could pretend nothing had changed. And that was my second mistake, because everything had changed. I told myself that the woman, Maria, who'd meant so much to you, didn't matter, that the terrible things you believed about me didn't matter, because the only thing I could think of was that you were back and you wanted me.' Angrily, she brushed at the tears coursing down her cheeks. 'What a fool I was—you see, I believed you. Someday, we can talk about what happened, you said. Forget the past, you said. But you never forgot, did you?' Her voice rose in anger and pain. 'The first time you found reason to doubt me, to distrust me, you did.'

He reached out towards her and touched her arm. 'Cat, if you'd only give me a chance ...'

'No,' she whispered, 'I won't. After all the things you said to me, do you really think you can just ... just walk in here and hand me an apology?' Her voice broke and she turned away from him. 'I loved you, Luke. But you don't even know what that means. Love is ... is trusting another person as much as you trust yourself. It's believing in them, no matter how tough that may be sometimes. It's what you build all your hopes and dreams on. But you . . .' She bowed her head and took a deep, shuddering breath. 'This is pointless. It's like a post mortem on one of the guinea-pigs in the lab. When it's finished, we'll know why it's dead, but it won't come back to life. Not ever, no matter what we do or say.'

'Caitlin . . .' he said brokenly, 'Caitlin . . .'

In one swift motion, she slipped past him to the cabin door. 'Please leave,' she murmured, not looking at him. 'That's the one thing you can do for me, Luke. Just go away and don't ever come back.'

He was beside her before she could move away, and his arms closed around her, drawing her body close against his.

'You don't mean that,' he said, and kissed her, his mouth as warm, as sweet as it had always been, as she would always remember it. She fought against the feelings his touch had brought to life, reminding herself that there was no going back, determined to protect the little pride she had left until at last, as she stood unmoving in his embrace, his arms fell away from her.

'Now will you leave?' she whispered.

He stared at her in silence while time and the world seemed to stand still, and then he nodded and pulled up the collar of his jacket.

'I don't blame you, Cat,' he said softly, turning towards the door. A sob rose in her throat as she saw his bowed head, his slumped shoulders, and her arms rose of their own volition, as if to call back what might have been and then fell, empty, to her sides. 'I just wish . . .' His words were lost in the sudden, wailing wind that almost wrenched the door from his grasp.

Rain pelted into the cabin, seeming to fall from the solid wall of white fog that had obliterated everything outside. Nothing was visible beyond the open door.

Even the path leading up the cliff seemed to have vanished behind the opaque curtain of the raging storm.

Angry despair washed over Caitlin. 'I asked you to leave an hour ago,' she muttered. 'Just look at what's happened to the weather. Now it's too late.'

Luke shrugged his shoulders and picked his cap up from the table. 'Don't worry about it, Cat. I'll manage.'

She slammed the door and walked across the cabin to the fireplace. 'Even if you managed to climb up to the road without falling off the cliff, you certainly couldn't go anywhere, not without killing yourself. And I don't need that on my conscience.' She took a deep breath and collapsed into the rocking chair. 'You can stay until this damned weather lifts.'

'Cat . . .'

'But I swear to you,' she said with quiet intensity, 'if you say another word, I'll go outside and sit in my car until the fog clears.'

He stared at her and then sank down on the narrow cot against the wall. She watched him warily for a minute, and then she reached behind her and drew a brightly coloured Navaho blanket from the back of the rocker. Wrapping it tightly around herself, she curled up in the chair, her feet tucked under her, listening to the keening moan of the wind outside the cabin and the splatter of rain pelting against the windows. Cautiously, from under lowered lashes, she peered over at Luke. He was slumped back against the wall, staring distantly at some time and place unknown to her.

She closed her eyes and turned her face away, determined not to look at Luke's dark, brooding face again. This man, whose love was all she had ever wanted in life, had returned to her, asking her to give him absolution for the wrongs he'd done her. As he had brought her grief, now he brought guilt and apology—everything, she thought, except love. How filled with bitter irony life was. In death, Justin had finally accomplished what he had been unable to do in life. His hand had reached from the grave to separate them.

There was an eerie, supernatural quality to the sound of the wind whipping through the redwoods above the cabin. It provided a mournful counterpoint to the pounding of the waves as they broke on the rocks far below. Caitlin burrowed deeper into the comforting warmth of the blanket. The storm was worse than had been predicted, she thought. It would be hours before Luke could leave. Then, she would pack the few things she needed and, at the first light of morning, she would leave for San José. She'd need only a day or two to collect her things and then... And then, where? Chicago, perhaps, or even Houston—there were lots of new businesses in Houston. Surely there would be a job there for her, a new life... Carefully, she risked a glance at Luke again. Perhaps someday she'd be able to think of him without feeling this terrible ache deep within her. Perhaps someday she'd remember only the good years they'd shared. It seemed a cold comfort, and she shivered at the thought of the bleak future stretching ahead. With a sigh, she drew the blanket up around her neck and rested her head against the back of the rocker.

CHAPTER FOURTEEN

CAITLIN struggled upwards from the depths of a deep, dream-filled sleep. Her eyes opened wide, but the little cabin was filled with unyielding darkness, save for the dying red embers in the fireplace. For a moment, she sat still, trembling with cold, trying to orient herself. A sound had awakened her, some soft noise in the blackness. She shifted uncomfortably, easing the stiffness in her back and legs, then rose and placed some logs and kindling in the hearth. Carefully, she coaxed the fire to life, eager to banish the shadows that lingered in the corners of the room. Suddenly, above the moan of the wind, she heard the sound that had awakened her again. At first it was a whisper, then an agonised cry, and she realised it was the drawn-out syllables of her own name that she heard, torn from Luke's throat. Quickly, she crossed the room to his side and knelt beside him on the soft rya rug.

'Luke,' she whispered, touching his shoulder, 'Luke ... what is it?'

He moaned and rolled away from her. She brushed the dark hair back from his damp forehead and leaned closer to him, the metallic taste of fear in her mouth.

'Luke, I'm right here. Please, wake up.'

'Cat?' he murmured thickly, turning towards her. 'Cat?' He reached out and grasped her shoulders. 'Oh, God, Cat. I was dreaming ... I was running down a trail through the jungle, and you were ahead of me, somewhere out there in the night, but I couldn't ...' His voice trailed off to a whisper and he shuddered. 'I couldn't find you, Cat. I called and I searched, but you were gone. You were gone, Cat. I . . .'

'Shhh,' she said softly. 'It's all right, Luke. Wait and I'll put on the lamp. It must have run out of fuel . . .'

'No!' The single word sounded as if it had been wrenched from him. He swung his legs around and sat up. 'Don't go away just yet, Cat,' he murmured, his fingers biting into her. 'Give me a minute. Just let me be sure . . .' His hands moved up her shoulders and touched her face. 'It's always the same dream,' he whispered. 'But this time I really found you. You're really here, by my side.' She drew in her breath as his fingers touched her cheeks. 'You're crying,' he said softly, as he felt the damp warmth of her tears. 'Cat, what is it?'

She shook her head and bit her lip. 'It's nothing,' she said, 'nothing. It's just . . . I . . . I thought something had happened to you.'

His laugh was like a cut-off cry of pain. 'What more could happen to me?' he said bitterly 'I've already lost you.'

'Luke, don't . . .'

'Don't stop me, Cat,' he murmured, cupping her face in his hands. 'I know you don't want to hear it, but I can't go on without telling you. I love you, Cat. I've never stopped loving you. And I need you. My life makes no sense without you.'

'Luke, please,' she whispered, trying to shut out the sound of his voice, steeling herself against the tremulous whisper of longing deep within her. 'Don't say these things. It's time we let go of the past and faced the future.'

'There is no future without you,' he said flatly. 'That's why I just couldn't handle it when I thought . . . I must have been out of my mind, Cat, to have believed you could have married Justin for any of the terrible things I accused you of. Hell, I know what he was like. Even when we were kids, he wanted whatever I had, just because it was mine. And he'd take it from me, any way he could. I had some stupid, idiotic idea he'd change, but I guess he never did. Over the years, I'd learned not to listen to half of what he said, especially about you, but when I told him I was going to marry you, make you my wife before I left on that trip, he hit all the right buttons and I let him talk me out of it. It all seemed so sensible, so logical. He said the trip might be dangerous, that it would be unfair to tie you to me. And I listened to him, Cat. "You're right, Justin," I said. "I've got to think of what's best for Caitlin. I'll wait until I get back."' His bitter laughter pierced the darkness. 'Well, I came back, all right. Except all I could think of was myself.'

'No,' she said quickly, her heart aching at the pain in his voice, 'don't say that. You couldn't help it. I should have realised what those years had done to you. I thought I had, but...'

'Don't make any more excuses for me,' he said sharply. 'The time I spent in that village was only one kind of hell, Cat, but there are others. Your life with Justin must have been hell, too.' He smoothed the hair back from her face and his fingers lingered lovingly on her skin. 'I still remember the way he used to look at you, as if he were a predator and you were the prey that always managed to keep just out of reach. I taxed him with it, a couple of times, and he just laughed at me, said you couldn't convict a man for his thoughts, only for his actions. I don't even know if it was you he wanted, or just a way to get at me. There was always something ... something twisted about Justin, even when we were kids, and it got worse when we started running the company together.'

Caitlin sighed and nodded her head. 'I knew how hard it was for you to work together. That was why I tried to talk you into selling the company that time.'

'I know, Cat. But Thomas meant so much to me, to my father... I offered to buy Justin out once, a long time ago, but he just laughed at me. He said he'd be damned if he'd leave me centre-stage with the Thomas name. So I kept telling myself he was my brother, the only real family I had left. How he must have hated me!'

'I don't think he really hated you, Luke. He hated what he thought you were. I think that's why he wanted to sell Thomas; maybe that's even why he wanted me, so he could destroy everything that reminded him of you.'

'I know that,' Luke murmured hoarsely. 'If only I'd listened to you in Paris...'

Caitlin choked back a sob. 'That's what I can't accept,' she whispered. 'If you'd loved me, really loved me...'

'Loved you?' he repeated, almost angrily. 'That's what this is all about, don't you see? I loved you so much that when I thought I'd lost you, there was nothing left but hate to fill the emptiness within me.' His fingertips moved gently across her face and wiped the tears from her eyes. 'Maybe I really was crazy,' he said softly. 'That's how I felt sometimes during the past four years, locked up in that stinking hut. It was like a nightmare you never wake up from. I was the enemy, and they never let me forget it. Your love was all I had to cling to, to give me the will to go on from one endless day to the next.'

She reached out to touch him, and his hand clasped hers tightly.

'You filled my days and nights with hope, Cat. When they beat me, when I wanted nothing more than the comfort of death, I'd think of you and I'd find the strength to survive. And when they finally eased up a little, you were the reason I risked an escape. Do you understand, Cat? You were all I lived for, and when I found out about you and Justin...' His voice broke and the sound of his ragged breathing seemed to fill the cabin. 'It wasn't a simple question of believing you, Cat,' he said finally in a whisper. 'I was like a man who'd built his life around a dream, and when that dream dissolved into the nightmare of what had happened. I just couldn't face it. And so I tried to make my own reality, and then when I heard about Clarke, all the demons I had tried to bury came back, and they tipped me over the edge. And all the time,' he said, his hand reaching for hers, 'I was blind to what you had done for me.'

Caitlin studied his face in the glimmering firelight. He seemed drawn and haggard, and she caught her breath as she realised how tenuous had been his hold on sanity, how fragile had been his will to survive during the long years of his captivity.

'It's all right, Luke,' she said softly. 'I have no regrets about what I did. It gave me a way to keep a part of you alive, and I would have died without that. I loved you so much...'

'You said you loved me, Cat. Does that mean it's gone? Have I killed your love forever?'

She reached out and touched his face with trembling hands. 'You can't destroy love so easily,' she said breathlessly, raising her face to his. 'Don't you know that by now?'

He bent over her and their lips met and clung together in the darkness.

'Cat,' he whispered hoarsely as he slipped to the floor and knelt beside her, 'I love you so much. Each time I thought of you and Justin together...'

'It was never like this with him,' she began, and he

placed his fingers gently across her mouth.

'I know that now,' he whispered. 'From this day forward, nothing matters except us.'

Again, his mouth covered hers, and she sighed as his arms drew her closer to him. 'You're right,' she said, her face buried in the crook of his shoulder. 'Nothing matters but us—not Justin, not Maria—are you laughing at me?' she demanded, trying to pull free of his embrace.

'About Maria,' he said, taking a deep breath.

'You don't have to say anything,' she said quickly. 'I understand. You thought you'd never get away. And she kept you alive, Luke. She...'

'She was seventy years old, she weighed fourteen stone, and she thought I looked like her dead grandson,' he said softly. 'Can you forgive me? I wanted to make you jealous, but I shouldn't have let you think there was anyone else. There never could be.' He paused and lifted her chin. 'Now who's laughing?' he said with mock indignation.

'I'm sorry,' Caitlin gasped. 'But if you knew the picture I've been carrying around in my head of Maria ... long black hair, voluptuous body, dark eyes...'

The laughter caught in her throat as his mouth brushed against her ear. 'Yours is the only picture I ever wanted,' he said huskily. 'Green eyes, the colour of the sea before a storm, brown hair gleaming like ripe chestnuts...' His hand touched the soft swell of her breast and she trembled. 'Sweet, soft curves that were meant to fit my hands and mouth...'

She sighed as his mouth descended on hers, and her lips parted under the gentle pressure of his. She felt the touch of his hand as his fingers opened the buttons of her cotton shirt and she arched her body against his, shameless in her eagerness to help him strip her of the clothing that separated them. The warm glow of the fire danced over them as her hands moved under his shirt, smoothing the silken skin across his back, lingering on the ridged muscles in his shoulders, then moving to the crisp hair on his chest. She murmured his name as he kissed the tender flesh behind her ear and, as his mouth travelled down her neck, inflaming her senses with love and desire, she wrapped her arms more tightly around him, wanting somehow to become one with him for all time.

'Caitlin,' he whispered. 'my only love. My forever love.'

His mouth moved gently, tenderly against hers, as if to savour the taste of her. She leaned back slowly, drawing him with her and when, suddenly, he pulled back, she shook her head fiercely.

'Don't stop,' she whispered, grateful for the fire glow that disguised the embarrassed blush she felt flaming across her cheeks. 'I love you so much, Luke. Make love to me, please.'

'I will,' he growled, 'but only if you agree to my price.' She drew a startled breath as she waited for his next words. 'Marry me, Caitlin,' he said, and a smile of joy lit her face. 'Tell me you'll fly to Nevada with me tomorrow and become my wife.'

'Are you sure?' she murmured, tears of happiness spilling from her eyes. 'You have to be sure, Luke.'

'I've always been sure of loving you,' he said simply. 'I loved you that summer you first came to work for me, when you were only seventeen. I loved you that day on the beach, just down the trail from here. I loved you that night in the château. I even loved you when I said all those ugly things to you that last, terrible night in Paris. And in between all those times, all the days and nights and minutes and seconds, Cat, I loved you. Please, darling, say that you'll marry me.'

'Yes,' she whispered, covering his face with kisses. 'Yes, yes, yes, oh Luke, my love, yes.'

Her whispered words were lost against the fierce, demanding pressure of his mouth on hers. With a muffled cry, Caitlin opened her mouth to his, returning his kisses with the pain born of years of waiting and despair. There was a hunger in her that only his lips could feed, an emptiness in her arms that only his body could fill. The touch of his hands on her was like a searing flame, and yet she could not get close enough to him to satisfy the love and need within her. She wanted to tell him she'd waited a lifetime for this moment, but words were impossible, meaningless symbols that drifted beyond reach in this sea of sensation and love. She strained against him, trying somehow to melt into his flesh. As if he knew her thoughts, her desires, he ran his hand over her body, touching her fevered skin with featherlike caresses, and when finally his fingers brushed over her ribs and touched her breast, Caitlin sighed with pleasure.

'Caitlin,' he whispered, 'Caitlin . . .'

She helped him take the open shirt from her shoulders, helped his strong hands ease her blue jeans down her legs, exulting in the strength of their need for each other. The touch of his mouth against the swell of her breast above her lace bra made her tremble and he paused, but she shook her head and clasped the back of his neck, urging his mouth downward, longing for the feel of it on her skin. At last, when he opened the clasp of her bra, when his gentle, soft touch caressed her naked breast, she cried out against his mouth. He drew back from her and then, with a groan, he bent his head and his lips found her taut, waiting flesh. Caitlin caught her breath and trembled like a leaf caught up in the storm that had reached a frenzied pitch outside the cabin.

Luke drew back and her hand reached out to him. 'I used to dream of making love to you, Cat,' he whispered, and she heard the soft, slapping sound of his shirt as he pulled it from him and tossed it aside. 'And now, the dream is real.' He traced his finger down her cheek, along her throat, down her breast, and she reached out and touched him, her hand moving tentatively over his bare chest. He caught her in his arms and brought her yielding body to his, so that her soft curves merged with the wonderful hardness of his lean, muscled body. His hands moved into the luxuriant thickness of her hair, drawing her head back so that the long, delicate column of her throat was bared to the flame that was his mouth. Slowly, his body urged hers down to lie on the soft rya rug, and then he was kissing her again, long, passionate kisses that filled her with the sweet, glorious taste of him. By the shadowed glow of dancing flames in the fireplace, Caitlin watched through half-closed eyes as Luke knelt above her, his hazel eyes dark with desire.

'I love you, Cat,' he murmured. 'I'll love you forever.'

She closed her eyes as his fingers closed on the lace edge of her panties and began to ease them down her hips.

'You're so beautiful,' he whispered throatily as he exposed her compliant body to his eyes. 'So lovely, Cat. Here,' he murmured huskily, touching his mouth softly to her breasts, 'and here,' he said, and his lips brushed across the rounded curve of her hip, 'and especially here.'

Caitlin gasped as his mouth found her tender, hidden self. 'Luke . . . my love . . .'

'Always,' he said fiercely, 'always.'

Her eyes opened wide as she heard the hiss of a zipper, and then he was beside her again, the heat of him burning against her.

'Never leave me,' she whispered, burying her face against his chest. 'Swear it to me.'

'I'll never leave you, darling,' he promised, and her heart filled with happiness at the sound of his words. 'From this day forward,' he murmured, as his hands stroked her in the age-old ritual of love.

Till death us do part, she thought, shuddering at the chilling memory of the day she'd been told he was lost to her forever. The sham that had been her brief, unhappy marriage rose up before her, and she pushed lightly against Luke's chest.

'Luke, wait...' She looked up into his face and took a deep breath. 'I have to tell you... about Justin and me...'

For a second, his eyes darkened with pain, and then he smiled at her. 'It doesn't matter, Cat,' he said tenderly. 'This is the beginning for us. Our love will make everything new.'

His mouth sought hers with an urgency that could no longer be denied as he gathered her to him, and the time for words was gone.

Caitlin's arms and heart opened to receive him. In the wonder of their joining, she forgot everything but her aching need to become part of his flesh. There was a brief, searing pain, and then Luke gasped and drew back from her.

'Caitlin,' he said in wonder and disbelief, 'dear God, Caitlin. Why didn't you tell me?'

'That's just what I was trying to do,' she whispered. 'But how...'

She sighed and stirred beneath him. With a groan, he pulled her to him.

'I didn't think you'd want to talk now,' she murmured shamelessly, and he gave himself up to what her hands and body were willing him to do.'

* * *

As the first faint touch of dawn filled the little cabin with its rosy glow, Luke stroked the hair back from Caitlin's flushed cheeks and smiled at her.

'If we don't get out of here quickly, we never will,' he teased. 'And I refuse to let another night go by without knowing we're husband and wife.'

Caitlin grinned and stretched lazily. 'Isn't it a perfect day for a wedding?' she asked happily. 'No more fog, no more storm—I can hardly wait until we get back from Nevada.'

Luke looked at her in surprise. 'I thought brides were supposed to look forward to their weddings. But here you are, on the morning of your wedding day, already wishing it was over.'

She blushed and looked away from him. 'I'm looking forward to it,' she said in a hushed voice. 'But I keep thinking of coming back to this cabin with you for a week.'

'Two weeks, at least,' he laughed, tweaking her nose. 'I'm going to carry you across that threshold, bar the door, board up the windows, and make love to you from morning to night.'

She blushed even harder. 'Would you believe three weeks?' she asked, and Luke burst out laughing and gathered her into his arms.

'Cat,' he said finally, 'about you and Justin . . . can you talk about it, or would you rather not?'

She nestled against him, safe and secure in his arms, and shook her head. 'No, it's all right now. I want you to know, Luke. He . . . before the wedding, each time he touched me, I did my best not to shudder. It didn't matter to him, he said. He knew how I felt—I made no pretence about it—and he swore that I'd change my mind about him, that I'd come to want him.' An icy chill ran through her and she shivered. 'I didn't, of course. If anything, once we were together, alone, with the bargain legalised, I only despised him all the more.'

'Cat, sweetheart, you don't have to tell me any more. I'm just so happy that he didn't . . . that I was the first man to make love to you . . .' He kissed her gently and she smiled up at him. 'At least there was some decency left in the man, after all.'

She hesitated briefly and then shook her head. 'I know you'd like to believe that,' she whispered, 'but that isn't quite the way it was. On our wedding night, when he came to my room . . . I started to cry when he touched me. I thought of how I'd longed to be with you that way, how now I'd never be with you, and I cried. Justin laughed at first, and then he became angry. He accused me of trying to make him into a villain . . .'

Luke snorted indignantly. 'Trying?' he said incredulously, his face whitening.

'And he said he wouldn't play into my hands, that he'd never had to force a woman before and he wasn't about to start with me. He stalked out in fury, and when he came to me the next night, the same thing happened all over again.'

'My poor darling,' Luke whispered, kissing the tears that had gathered on her lashes. 'You must have been terrified.'

'I was,' she admitted in a small voice, 'especially when he finally said my "act" was overdone, that it wasn't going to stop him from collecting what he was entitled to. And so I resigned myself to it, I told myself that he was right, that I'd . . . I'd contracted to be his wife. And then I didn't cry, I didn't even flinch. But . . . but Justin . . . Justin couldn't do anything. He flew into a rage, said it was my fault, that it was my coldness that caused it.' Caitlin shuddered and buried her face against Luke's shoulder. 'I don't know, maybe it was true. He used to boast to me about all his other women... All I know is that it happened each time he... During the day, I did all the right things, I was the wife he wanted me to be, but at night, when we were alone... It was terrible,' she whispered, 'terrible. Eventually, he stopped coming to my bedroom at all. Sometimes I felt ... almost guilty, because we'd made a deal, you see, and I intended to keep my part of it, no matter how awful...'

She began to sob and Luke held her against him, stroking her tenderly until at last she sighed and wiped her eyes.

'Listen to me, Caitlin,' he said firmly, tilting her face up to his. 'You more than fulfilled your end of the deal. You lived with him, you took his name, you went wherever he went. God knows he wasn't entitled to as much of you as he had. Perhaps, in some strange way he never understood, he couldn't bring himself to take something that could never really be his. Whatever the reason, it's all behind us now.'

'Yes,' she said thankfully, smiling at him, 'it is, isn't it? We have a lifetime ahead of us.'

Luke bent his head and kissed her. 'You're wonderful, Cat. How can I ever repay you for all you've done for me?'

Caitlin grinned mischievously and blushed. 'When we get back after our wedding,' she purred softly, 'I'll think of something.'

From *New York Times* Bestselling author Penny Jordan, a compelling novel of ruthless passion that will mesmerize readers everywhere!

Penny Jordan
Silver

Real power, true power came from Rothwell. And Charles vowed to have it, the earldom and all that went with it.

Silver vowed to destroy Charles, just as surely and uncaringly as he had destroyed her father; just as he had intended to destroy her. She needed him to want her... to desire her... until he'd do anything to have her.

But first she needed a tutor: a man who wanted no one. *He* would help her bait the trap.

Played out on a glittering international stage, Silver's story leads her from the luxurious comfort of British aristocracy into the depths of adventure, passion and danger.

AVAILABLE NOW!

SIL-1A

You'll flip . . . your pages won't!
Read paperbacks *hands-free* with

Book Mate • I

The perfect "mate" for all your romance paperbacks

Traveling • Vacationing • At Work • In Bed • Studying • Cooking • Eating

Perfect size for all standard paperbacks, this wonderful invention makes reading a pure pleasure! Ingenious design holds paperback books OPEN and FLAT so even wind can't ruffle pages—leaves your hands free to do other things. Reinforced, wipe-clean vinyl-covered holder flexes to let you turn pages without undoing the strap...supports paperbacks so well, they have the strength of hardcovers!

Pages turn WITHOUT opening the strap

SEE-THROUGH STRAP

Reinforced back stays flat

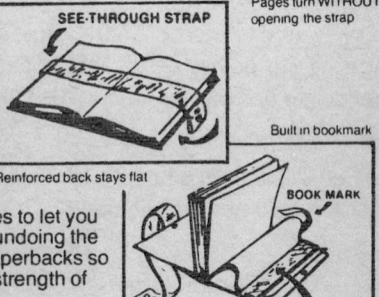

Built in bookmark

BOOK MARK

BACK COVER HOLDING STRIP

10 x 7¼, opened
Snaps closed for easy carrying, too

Available now. Send your name, address, and zip code, along with a check or money order for just $5.95 + .75¢ for delivery (for a total of $6.70) payable to Reader Service to:

Reader Service
Bookmate Offer
3010 Walden Avenue
P.O. Box 1396
Buffalo, N.Y. 14269-1396

Offer not available in Canada
*New York residents add appropriate sales tax.